JOYRIDE

WHEN LOYALTY KILLS

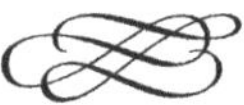

PENNY BLACWRITE

JESSICA WATKINS PRESENTS

First edition

❀ Created with Vellum

DEDICATION

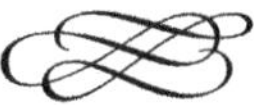

If you only knew the pain I endured and relived to write this book, you'd truly be blown away. It took a lot of courage to just bear it all. All Praise goes to God, the Father and my Lord & Savior Jesus Christ. Thank you for your grace and strength.

This book is dedicated to the three women who shaped my foundation as a young girl — Mommy, Auntie, and my grandmother — who I'm named after — Pamela.
Thank you, Kathryn O'Dell — my #1 editor and the first woman who inspired me to write books for a living.

Thank you to all of my line sisters — especially Cynthia (Break of Dawn), Kira "Buddy" (Inception), Dom (Orion's Belt), Angela (Insomnia), and most importantly, Cassidy, my back (Twilight)— for inspiring me to incorporate your line names as themes that relate to my personal story.

Last but not least, thank you to my best bih, Kida for always supporting and believing in me.

CHAPTER 1

BREAK OF DAWN

An event or occurrence that brings light and positivity to many bleak situations. But like the break of dawn, you sometimes have to arise from a dark place of negativity, whether it was brought on by others or your own perceptions.

Just last month, I called it quits with Clyde, for certain this time! His actions were the ultimate betrayal and violation of not only my trust, but my daughter's safety as well.

"She's just a baby!" rings through my mind every time I think of the innocence he took and the fire he ignited in her impressionable spirit.

I remember it vividly. It was in the wee hours of the morning in mid-June, around 4am. The steaming humidity throughout the night became thicker and thicker — signifying that we were in for an unbearably hot summer indeed. But it wasn't just the stifling air that kept me up that night. I was overwhelmed with excitement. My baby girl, Nia, was stepping up from elementary school, and her graduation was set to start in just a few hours.

As I was about to doze off, Nia, awkwardly tall and chunky for a twelve-year-old, ran into my bedroom, startled.

The salty tears stained her pretty face as water gushed from her eyes. Choked by hysteria, she struggled to speak. Instead, her cries spoke to me. She belted out a few moans in between unclear words, heavy breathing, and hyperventilation.

Initially, I was confused because Clyde just checked her breathing and said her chest was clear of any wheezing.

Please, don't let my baby girl be sick on her big day, I thought and sighed to myself.

"Can I talk to you, Mommy?" she asked, fighting back the tears. "Out there," she said, pointing to the door.

I got out of bed, grabbed baby girl by the hand, and rushed out of my bedroom. We scurried into our small bathroom, which usually felt quaint and peaceful, but the olive-green walls were spinning as I asked,

"What's wrong, baby?"

"Clyde touched me."

At the sound of those words, my mind went blank, and my fleeting soul turned black as my body drifted away on a dreamy cloud.

Nia stood in shock as she looked at me. At that moment, I could see her fear, and I could feel the brewing trauma fester in her pretty little soul. Exhausted and embarrassed, I refused to call the cops. It was after 4am and we had to be up in the next three hours to get ready for Nia's graduation.

I'll handle it tomorrow. Everything. Even Clyde. As of now I just need to hold my composure.

"Nia, babygirl, stay right here for one minute."

I rushed out of the bathroom where I left Nia and opened the door to the bedroom I shared with Clyde. As soon as I entered the room his nervous glare shifted to me instantly.

"Sleep on the couch tonight! Nia's gonna sleep in here with me."

Unfazed, Clyde started to gather his pillows and an extra comforter and headed out of the bedroom. I ran to get Nia from the bathroom and held her tight.

"Babygirl don't worry. Let's get some sleep. Tomorrow is your big day. Don't you worry about a thing. We'll handle it tomorrow.

Terribly afraid, she grabbed my hand and followed me into the bedroom. I did not want to fight with Clyde. Not because I was scared of him, but because I was done. There was nothing he could say. I had no questions or comments, just demands that would be dealt with shortly the very next morning.

* * *

THE NEXT FEW hours proved to be my most critically acclaimed performance. We got dressed in our matching lavender outfits to celebrate Nia's biggest achievement, her first graduation.

While faking a smile for not only the public, but also relatives, I was steaming with hatred. Refusing to display just a bit of anger for any of the hundred people to witness, I grabbed Nia tight as we both hid the horror in our hearts while posing in a chummy photo with Clyde.

Dressed uncomfortably in my fitted suit, I was sweating profusely. The sweating tripled because despite how emotional I was, I rose to the occasion. The effort to save face and mask my feelings showed up as light musk and a wet spot on the underarm of my suit jacket. While the photographer snapped the portrait, I whispered in Nia's ear. "Don't you worry, babygirl. It will be all over soon."

Nia didn't respond but forced a grin for the flash as she tightly clung on to my waist.

As much as I wanted the day to end before it even got started, I was determined to celebrate with Nia. She didn't need to see her Mommy angry, and she didn't need to worry about Clyde.

As soon as we finished taking photos, I shooed Nia away to our relatives as I pulled Clyde to the side. His sweaty face reeked of pity as he hung his head low, too embarrassed to look me in the eye.

"You are no longer welcome in my house, starting today. Don't worry about your clothes or any knick knacks. I will drop everything off to your mother's by the end of the week."

The sun was beaming directly on us, so I didn't wait for Clyde to pick his head up and face me. I slowly turned my back to him and began walking. Within three steps, Clyde's words echoed loudly throughout the parking lot for all to hear.

"I'M SORRY, JOI."

I was so far gone mentally that I refused to address him with a response, so I whispered to myself.

"And a sorry man is the last thing I want."

Clyde was the only man I had been with for the last eleven years, so breaking up with him left me with mixed emotions. On one hand, I felt vindicated because finally I had a reason to leave, but on the other hand, I was disappointed. Although the relationship had grown stale and stagnant over the years, the last thing I expected Clyde to do was molest my daughter, who he'd raised from a toddler, after Nia and I were both released from prison.

But ultimately, it was my fault for putting anything past a man, especially an ex-crack addict. To face the realization that I allowed a relationship with a man I never genuinely wanted in the first place to not only persist for eleven years, but to endanger the welfare of my daughter as well, was by far the greatest disappointment I'd experienced in a while.

The most disheartening reality of all is that had Clyde's perversion not expedited our breakup, I probably would have been stuck with him. They say everything happens for a reason, but it was hard to settle with the fact that my revival into true womanhood would change the trajectory of not only my life but Nia's also.

CHAPTER 2

REMINISCENCE

recall to mind of a long-forgotten experience or fact, the process or practice of thinking or talking about past experiences.

When I was released from prison eleven years ago, Clyde was there for me and my baby. He was our sole provider. Young and with child, I came home to nothing. My mother, Pam, sold everything I stole and bought for Nia. At the time I got locked up, I was eight months pregnant. It was December 1995, and a blistering cold storm had just subsided, yet some ice still paved the ground.

Since my belly was so big and accompanied by swollen feet, I slowed down on my daily store visits. Before that day, I hadn't boosted in about two months. My gut feeling told me to stay in, but I just couldn't say no to my best friend and the sweet steals awaiting me.

"Girl! It's sweet as hell in A&S right now. They got all the baby shit. You ain't even gotta boost today. Just come with me and go shopping.

I know you be spending money on that baby like crazy," she said before laughing and rubbing my tummy.

"You know it! Racked up nice. My baby got three strollers, tons of Johnson & Johnson lotion and wipes, and new clothes stacked up from wall to wall in my room."

Stealing everything was impossible, so I lifted the necessities — which were normally smaller and easier to get away with — and used one of my many credit cards or paid cash for expensive purchases like a $1600 Bugaboo stroller that my baby girl just had to have.

"I know that's right. Well, hurry up! Let's go. I got us a ride up to the Bronx," she said with a sense of urgency.

"Go get dressed!" she demanded.

Considering that I didn't need to lift anything in particular for a customer, the plan was to actually go shopping that day, which I did, but as soon as my boosting buddy got caught, I was swept up with her. Guilty by association.

Sitting inside the cold and dreary holding cell in the precinct with only my belly to rub and myself to hug, my head hung low in defeat.

The officer who arrested me approached the cell and banged his baton loudly against the bars. White, tall, and a bit stocky, I can still make out his face today. He had a scar on his nose that I'd never forget.

"Holloway. You've got five warrants out for your arrest—three for shoplifting and the other two are for fake checks. The judge's gonna have a field day with you," he said in between two obnoxious laughs.

The asshole officer wasn't lying either. Even after pleading not guilty, due to my excessive number of warrants, I was sentenced to three years, which eventually got reduced to eighteen months in Rose M. Singer Center, the only female jail on Rikers Island.

It was official — I'd be having my baby in jail.

* * *

ON THE DAY I gave birth while lying in the bed at Elmhurst Hospital, I fixated my stare on the fluttering snow flurries dancing outside of the window. Watching the never-ending whiteness in the air blocked out the combination of contraction pain and the bruising from the tightness of the handcuffs that straddled me to the bed rail. The stark brightness of the hospital lights blinded me as I fought hard to not pass out while delivering my baby.

They would love to see it. But I be damned if I let these grimy CO bitches watch me give up.

Irritated and in agonizing pain, I screamed with fury, "GET THESE OFF OF ME NOW! LET ME DELIVER MY BABY

IN PEACE!" Erratically, I began banging my hands on the rail, trying to loosen the shackles from my wrists, but nothing worked.

Not even requests from the doctor or the tears from his assisting nurse made a difference.

Perplexed, yet still trying to maintain some form of professionalism, the doctor turned to the two police officers, who were standing in the room near the door and asked,

"Are those really necessary?"

"Absolutely necessary, Doctor. All inmates must be handcuffed when out of the facility. Unfortunately, even when giving birth," the officer responded sarcastically.

Disgusted, the doctor turned his back to the officers and continued to focus his attention on me.

"Gimme a push and another push and one more push." His voice sounded like a song in my dazed recollection.

I strained my pelvic as I continued to push to no avail. This baby was stubborn and she didn't want to come out. I placed both hands on the bed rails to give myself leverage to push harder.

"Oh God. Please let her come out," I begged in agony.

As I continued to grab hold of the bedrails, I was reminded of the handcuffs on my left wrist.

Finally after an hour of pushing, Nia came shooting out, and the nurse grabbed her tiny body to cut the umbilical cord. The nurse proceeded to wipe off the placenta from Nia's small, infant back as I laid winded and exhausted from pushing so hard. Nonetheless, I still held my hands out in anticipation to hold my baby. The nurse gently placed Nia in my arms, and the lingering baby smell mesmerized me as I looked into her big, beautiful brown eyes.

"You are my sunshine. My only sunshine. You make me happy when skies are grey. You'll never know, dear, how much I love you. Please don't take my sunshine away."

I planted at least twenty kisses on Nia and held her so tight as I hummed the sweet and soft lullaby. Just as I started to get comfortable with my baby's scent, a sudden doom came over me as I heard the rattle of the police officer's keys.

"Inmate. It's time to go."

"Just one more minute," I demanded.

Without even addressing my request, the short, overweight police officer turned to the nursing staff and said, "Nurse, please take the baby so we can transport the inmate back to the facility."

I refused to let go. I wanted my baby next to me.

"Don't worry, Holloway. You're in the prison nursery program. You'll see your baby as soon as possible."

Yet, soon wasn't soon enough for me.

The police officer's voice became muffled leaving me deaf as I watched her snatch Nia from my arms and hand her to the nurse as she and her colleague prepared to bus me back to Rikers.

Although jail wasn't by any means comfortable, the nursery didn't look much different from the comfort of one's home. Bright lights and bold colors dawned on the room where my joyful infant baby bounced up and down and struggled to walk and talk. I was allowed to visit her for a period throughout the day, in between my daily assigned jail work and group therapy. I spent that time reading to Nia and showering her with a sea of kisses and hugs.

Thinking back on it now, it was truly a blessing to have the privilege to bond with my baby the first year and a half. Most people would say that prison is no place to conceive a child, let alone raise one in. But Afeni Shakur did it, and Nia was my Tupac baby. Judge me all you want, but it is important for a child to spend the first year of their life with their mother.

Nia's dad, my baby daddy, was furious. On the few occasions he visited me, he begged to take Nia.

"Trust me. I'm her father. I won't let anything bad happen to her, Joi. Just let me take her. A baby doesn't belong here."

"Take her where? You don't even have a crib. Where my baby gon' sleep at?"

"Come on, girl. You know between my mother's and sister's, there's plenty of space and love for our baby."

"Boy, please. Your shiftless ass mother ain't even raise you, and you think you gon' take my baby and dump her off with some strangers while you run the streets? I think the fuck not. Where I come from, all the women in my family raise their own kids. We don't send our kids off to live with other people while we figure it out. We tough it out with our kids! My mother raised me, and I'm set on my decision — my baby gon' be right here with her mother where she belongs."

Angry and upset, he shook his head and gripped his lip tight.

"Watch and see. You gon' regret this shit." He got up from his seat and ended the visit.

For the remainder of my bid, I never saw him again, but I wasn't worried. Within a matter of weeks, Clyde replaced him. Indefinitely! I met Clyde through my best friend. He was her baby father's uncle. He always had a crush on me, but I ignored his advances. As soon as he heard I was locked up, he came to my aid when I needed him, and he took care of me and Nia inside of those hell walls and outside in the world, the devil's playground.

Clyde was a helping hand who turned into my man because of how good he treated me. Clyde visited twice a week and always kept my commissary full of money. Anything that Nia needed, she had. As soon as we came home, Clyde also put us up in an apartment that was fully furnished. Since my mother sold all of the clothes and strollers I had for Nia, he replaced them. Truly heaven-sent, Clyde rescued me at a time when I had no one.

Standing at only 5'3", he was fat and stocky with a protruding beer belly. Heavy in stature but light to the ear, Clyde's footprints barely whispered. His experience as a street boxer made it impossible to hear him sneak up on you. He wore braids and the latest urban gear, thanks to me. Sporting a beard was not his style, so he regularly shaved, which left his face and chin discolored and full of razor bumps.

Although I grew to love Clyde, he was never my type. The most I could do was dress him up. The worst of it all was that I could barely have a sensible conversation with him. Fueled by jealousy and rage, he couldn't handle the fact that I was constantly motivated to change my current situation. Before getting arrested, I had already made up my mind that I was not going to be a full-time booster. I had watched all the older women who taught me the reins lose everything — their homes, cars, jewelry, and most importantly, their zeal and vigor for a different and better life.

Once I was released, I was determined to get my shit together. My original plan was to attend Dudley, a cosmetology school in North Carolina. My mentor, who I met in jail, had everything set up; room and board and tuition were covered, but all I could hear were the words of my mother.

"Hairstylists don't make no money. You need a job."

So, I took up Accounting instead and decided to stay in New York, where I got caught up with Clyde. Just trying to survive turned into eleven years of confusion, drama, and stagnation.

Clyde had what you call stinkin' thinking. I could get his support on anything crooked or criminal. He'd knock a nigga out for me or hustle on the corner and bring home thousands, but he wouldn't commit to a nine to five simply because of the expected responsibility and structure. Nonetheless, I stopped caring and trying to coach Clyde. As long as the money came in, I refused to fight with him about his future. I certainly couldn't care less now.

It saddened me to learn that Clyde could raise a little girl as his own daughter then grope her as soon as she began to sprout. All I could think about was, *what if she hadn't told me? Would he have tried more?* Just thinking of it brought hatred to my soul. Disappointment filled my heart and rage was behind the fury in my eyes as I thought about how Clyde betrayed me.

Disheartened, I was prepared to pick up and keep pushing. With Clyde being gone everything relied on me — all the bills, all the chores and even the responsibility of caring for Nia solely on my own. I was accustomed to Clyde's contributions over the years and relied on him. With Nia growing older and now on her way to middle school, she required more of my attention, time, and money. Truthfully, I didn't know how I was going to manage all of this, but I'd be damned if I allowed a pedophile in my house just for some extra change. I wasn't raised like that. My momma ain't put no man over me, and I vowed to never do it to my daughter.

CHAPTER 3

RESTART

to start anew, to resume (something, such as an activity) after interruption.

P**resent Day – July 12, 2005**

Coming out of the local fruit stand into a dark, windy, starry night with two bags of groceries after a long day of work, I paused at the corner to light a cigarette. I took four long pulls and flicked it. I was trying to quit, but it was such a nasty habit to kick.

It was a humid night in early July, about two weeks after Nia's graduation. As I proceeded to cross the street, I was stopped by a white Lincoln Navigator on the way to my car. My hands began to tremble as the window slowly rolled down and revealed a glaring shadow of his face. The darkness of the sky made it difficult to make out the depth of his facial features.

Nonetheless, I could tell he was tall from the inside.

"Wah gwan babes," he muttered in a low yet sexy and intense tone. The Jamaican accent came to my surprise.

"Come up out of that car if you wanna talk to me," I spat back.

Honestly, I was scared. It was late, dark, and near my old neighborhood, a notorious housing project complex in Bed Stuy. Growing up in Brevoort Houses groomed me to be leery of any suspicious van, truck, or car that approached me. He flashed his signal and pulled around to my beat-up Nissan Altima, where my entire bumper was off, and the engine peeked through.

He put the car in park, opened the door, and stepped out of the vehicle in one instant motion, legs first and no struggle at all. He stood with a quiet strength, peering down at me from his 6'5" stature. I'm a measly short thing, standing at only 5'1". He nodded his head and pointed at me with his lips. He wore long dreadlocks that were proportionately sized, not the big freeform locks that most people disliked. Nevertheless, they complemented his chocolate hue and rugged style.

"Gal yuh sweet. I'm Tony Skank. What's your name, Princess?" he asked.

It came as a pleasant surprise to see Tony handle my feistiness with such unbothered indifference. It didn't scare him or intimidate him. He was so secure in his manhood that he didn't need to check me or show me who's boss. Yelling, cursing, or replying in a slick manner was unnecessary and a waste of time. His calmness instantly rubbed off on me. I didn't have to go there with Tony. He understood that ultimately arguing and testing a woman didn't serve him well in achieving his goal.

"Joyce, but call me Joi."

"Joy, Oh, Joy. Oh, yuh bring mi joy," he belted out in between a shy chuckle.

My eyes lit up as my smile began to widen, revealing my slight overbite that I'd developed as a kid from sucking my thumb. Braces were always an option, but I felt that my small gap complemented the overbite, making it less noticeable. The good thing was that I had stopped sucking my thumb years back, so the damage was somewhat reversing, definitely subsiding. Unconsciously, I raised my hand to my face, attempting to hide the fact that I was indeed trying to cover my flawed smile.

Tony took my hand into his and pulled me closer. In that instant, my head laid on his stomach, not too far from his chest where I heard his heart grow a stronger beat by the second. Knots in my stomach persisted as he wrapped his arms around me. Unknowingly to us both, our bodies were magnetically joined through a strong yet silent craving for one another. I looked up at him in awe, just happy to be with a man I was completely attracted to. Appreciating all of his physicality was an easy thing to do. I didn't have to squint or tilt my head to look at him. I could stand tall with pride and look him in the eye. At first sight, he was a stranger, but instantly I felt comfortable as if I had known him for years.

The truth was, I didn't expect to meet Tony just two weeks after putting Clyde out. In fact, I wasn't looking to meet anyone. I gave Clyde eleven of my best years, and at thirty-one, I knew I wanted something different, and I had to be intentional about who I spent my time with. I'd always been attracted to older guys, so I wasn't surprised to find out that Tony was forty-three — one of the only things he and Clyde had in common.

Other than that, I could already tell they were nothing alike. In less than five minutes, I instantly felt safe in Tony's embrace yet Clyde constantly kept me in strife and on guard about the stupidest things. His insecurities were through the roof. The truth is I never cheated on Clyde. I didn't really have to. Financially, he was a provider and personally, the sex was amazing. We'd argue here and there but I became immune to his stupidity. All I had to do was curse him out and it would subside momentarily. Our arguments were generally about silly childish things. More than not, Clyde was the one to usually start them. He created issues about any and everything insignificant.

With that chapter now being closed, I was finally free. Free to be and free to start over. Although I tried to resist it, I just knew I would be starting over in the hands of a new man.

CHAPTER 4

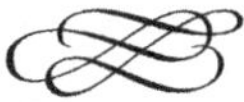

FAST-TAILED

"Fast (pronounced fass) tailed (or tail in some dialects) girl" is a term used mostly by Black women to describe young black girls who "intentionally demonstrate the carnal behaviors reserved for a woman beyond her years."

At only twelve years old, Nia was full-figured and curvy. We wore almost the same size — me an 18/20 and she, a 16. Although womanly in shape, she had a baby face, and I just prayed that it saved her from the predators of the street. Hopefully, they'd see her innocence and lack of experience and get deterred. Her chubby cheeks resembled a caricature of Fat Albert — round, plump, and ready to be popped. If you didn't see the baby in her face, you had to be blind.

This explains why I caught Nia talking to grown men on a chat line. They didn't have to see her adolescent face, although I don't know how they couldn't hear the immaturity in her voice. Things were spiraling so fast, and it became apparent that Nia really needed me. The last thing I needed was a distraction, but Tony kept calling and insisting we go out, and as much as I resisted, I felt a satisfied glee whenever his name popped up on my caller ID. This time was no exception. My blue Razr flip-phone began to vibrate. Reluctantly, I picked up on the third ring.

"Miss Joi. Mi need fuh git a bite ah yuh."

I chuckled two times before I spoke into the phone.

"Hello, Mr. Tony Skank," I crooned back coyly.

"Babylove, mi wah fuh c yuh."

"Oh, baby, trust me I know. But I'm busy for the next two weeks," I said, lying.

I wasn't busy, but I damn sure wasn't easy.

Within seconds, my house phone began to ring. The obnoxious and pestering ringtone startled me. Before I could tell Tony to hold on, he must have heard it for himself.

"Yuh real busy gal mi see. Mi call yuh later." Before I knew it, the line went blank.

I ran to my living room in search of the phone. I grabbed it on the last ring.

"Hello," I said into the phone, out of breath.

I heard a deep male voice on the next end.

"Hey, momma, this is Terrance; you gave me your number on the Chatline."

"Chatline? Who are you looking for?"

"Your name is Nia, right?" he questioned.

All of the rage I'd festered up towards Clyde a few weeks back was now shifting to Nia. My pressure skyrocketed while my blood felt like it was boiling. My eyes began to bulge because I simply wanted to understand. Not only was Nia craving the opposite sex, but she was also craving grown men. Why wasn't she playing double dutch with the other girls?

Luckily, I got rid of Clyde immediately. Before this incident happened, Nia wasn't on chatlines or thinking about boys — definitely not older men. What did I do to create this? When I was her age, I was in choir practice and on the cheerleading team amongst other girls. As much as I tried to acclimate Nia in a social environment, she always retreated. She would withhold and withdraw herself from her peers. In my eyes, she was shy and reserved. So, what possessed her to call a chatline and pretend to be older to speak with men? I swear, I would have rather dealt with a nappy-headed rug rat or even a teenage boy.

"How old are you, sir?" I asked.

"I'm thirty-six, ma. How old are you?" he responded.

"Twelve. I'm only twelve fucking years old."

"What? Twelve? Stop playing, ma. You said you were twenty-one," he said jokingly.

"My daughter is twelve fucking years old. Don't call my phone again, or I'm calling the cops," I screamed, before throwing the phone across the room.

I was livid, but Nia and I were going to get down to the bottom of it. My rage turned into disappointment. *What do I do? Beat her? Cry? Punish her?*

* * *

SOME THINGS I just didn't have all the answers to. Some things I just couldn't handle alone, but I thanked God that I always had a mother to confide in. Whether she was shooting dope or lighting a pipe, I could get a good word from Pam. And I was confident that the majority of whatever she had to say was rational and logical.

Back when I was a teenager and Pam was getting high, she was functional for many years. She maintained her city job at Harlem Hospital while using until things just spiraled out of control. However, she carried herself with so much class. Her light sing song sway was full of grace and precision. Carefully placing each foot in front of the other and making sure to never slouched, Pam stood with grandeur.

She spoke so eloquently and never cursed, but her choice of words would cut you. She had the perfect receptionist voice. Many times, when I was younger, my friends thought Pam was a white woman.

"Just because I have a decent vocabulary doesn't mean I sound like a white woman," she'd say in a sassy tone.

This was the Bajan in her. The feisty, sassy, educated slave who spoke the best English in the world, the Queen's English. That was the attitude of most Bajans.

Born in Barbados, my mother came to the U.S. at the age of five. Her mother, my grandmother, never took her back to visit as an older child. Therefore, Pam wasn't exposed to the culture and ultimately never got the opportunity to pass it down to me and my sister, Gloria. My grandmother traveled to Barbados at least once a year and left my mother home. She kept us far away from her culture.

"Don't you tell nobody you're from Barbados! These Americans don't like us," my grandmother told my sister and me as little girls.

"Besides, you guys aren't from Barbados anyway; you were born here in the U.S. But still, keep it to yourself!" she snapped.

My grandmother would sharply cut her eyes to me first, then quickly to my sister, usually with a smug grimace and emotionless stare. The annoying *psst* she made with her teeth sounded like a screeching train that would never come to a stop. As soon as it did, she gulped up the slimy remnants of okra soup from her bowl.

She continued to stare us down, darting her attention between my sister and me as she licked the okra slime off of her fork. It was the texture that always disgusted me. Cut into dime-sized pieces, the prickled okra would slither in a pool of green juice, hiding and waiting to be picked up and sucked on. As a kid, I refused to eat it.

My refusal was always followed by a slick, critical comment.

"You kids don't eat anything. That's why I can't take you anywhere."

I truly believed her until I got older and realized that we didn't fit into her perfect little world, and that shame was the real reason she never took us anywhere. She was so ashamed of Pam's drug addiction that she just left us alone — alone and isolated in her heart. She had a spot for us; it just wasn't a soft, tender spot.

However, Pam differed. I knew that there was nothing I could ever do to change how Pam loved me, and most importantly, how she showed it. More than anything, now and more than ever before, I needed my mother's love. Normally, I went to her strictly for dating advice, but when Nia developed her menstrual cycle two years back, I relied on Pam for a lot of parenting and mother-daughter counsel.

So, I decided to take the next afternoon off to pick Pam up from work. There was no need to call because I knew her schedule and most of her whereabouts. I made it to the quiet area of Spring Creek, located behind the Gateway Mall section of Brooklyn a little before 3pm.

I sat in my car, patiently allowing my cigarette to burn as I contemplated on whether or not I was done with my dose of cancer for the day. Disgusted with myself, instead of stubbing the bud into the ashtray, I flicked it out of my window. As soon as I looked up, I saw Pam, thick and plump, slowly gallivanting from her patient's home towards the parking lot. Her co-worker normally dropped her off at home because they live so close to each other.

Before she could make it to the curbside, I beeped my horn, belting out a loud honk. Pam turned her head in my direction, and her face lit up with joy. I shifted my gear into drive and sped up a few inches towards her and unlocked the door. She opened it gleefully, surprised to see me.

"Sista Suki. What are you doing over here?" she asked before getting in.

Despite how many years Pam spent drugging, her Hershey-kissed mocha skin was still soft, tight, and supple as a baby's butt. The toasty smell of cocoa butter that I remember as a child still lingered on her whenever she moved just an inch. The aroma instantly hit my nostrils as she settled in the car.

After attending a drug program and getting clean, Pam slowly regained her independence. It was like a baby learning how to walk, yet I was witnessing my mother start all over. Still, Pam put up a good fight to maintain her vanity. She was delicate by sight but strong in withstanding might. Even after birthing three kids, she had no stretch marks or facial wrinkles.

She was old school, and some things just didn't change. She still accented her daily baths with a capful of Jean Nate After Body Splash, and she still wore her signature red lipstick. Although she put on some pounds over the years, she still had no stomach due to all of the weight distributing to her ass. Since she started back working, she always kept her hair done, experimenting with different variations of blonde. Truth was, Pam barely missed a beat.

"Ma, I feel like I'm losing it. Nia's on chatlines talking to older men. She got niggas calling my house. This is getting outta hand. I don't know what to do." My voice was cracking, and I was pleading for a solution.

Pam chuckled in between two breaths as I began to drive off.

"So, that's what these kids are doing these days? On chatlines?"

That was not the response I expected at all. She almost sounded like she didn't care, so I remained quiet, which produced a long pause. She interrupted the awkward silence after a minute and asked,

"How old was the man?"

"Does it fucking matter? He was over eighteen. Nia's twelve."

I glanced to the right of me and noticed that Pam was snacking on some candy corn. The sucking sound she made with her tooth irritated the shit out of me.

"Well, it depends. Did she lie about her age? 'Cause what does a grown man want with a twelve-year-old? I mean, she is developed like you and me, so perhaps."

She paused again, this time as if she was at a loss for words.

"Listen! It don't matter how old the nigga was. Nia shouldn't be on my phone talking to no grown ass man."

"That's right. That's right. You right about that," Pam responded. She was starting to piss me off because she was not helping.

"Sista Suki, look here. Don't worry. She's not having sex yet, so you still got the control. You wasn't perfect, and Nia won't be either. This is only the beginning, but it's gon' be alright."

"Respectfully, Pam, I was not talking to no grown ass men at twelve. I was at the nursery with Daddy."

"Exactly! You and Gloria were in trusted hands. Nobody ever touched you, right?"

As soft and nonconfrontational as Pam's tone was, it still darted me in the heart. She was right. No matter how much partying, drugging, fighting, or tugging Pam and my Daddy did, they made sure we were safe and in the company of responsible adults.

Once my parents divorced, Daddy got remarried to his new wife, Louise, and moved south to Virginia when I was sixteen. On the other hand, Pam kept her boyfriends out of the house. Truthfully, we never had a stepfather.

Even when Pam remarried our little brother's father, he posed no threat. Pam and Bobby got married while he was incarcerated about two years after my brother was born.

Since Bobby spent most of my adult life in prison, he was never in the house with me and my sister as adolescents. Therefore, Pam didn't have to worry about her man touching us.

It was easy for Pam to judge. She didn't know what it was like to have to rely on another man to help you take care of your daughter. She had an ex-husband and an extended family that played an integral role in raising us — not to mention, she had Bobby, a real OG up north, holding things down financially. She just didn't understand.

To mask my feelings, I quickly changed the subject.

"How's Bobby, ma?"

"His old crazy ass is doing good. Just sent him a letter and shipped him some food during my lunch break."

CHAPTER 5

DISCIPLINE

control gained by enforcing obedience or order training that corrects, molds, or perfects the mental faculties or moral character

"You're to come straight home after school. No phone. No TV, and no hanging out. You are gonna spend some time reading the African American Almanac and the Bible. Your first assignment will be to read the story of Job and write me a report on the main lessons that Job learned. Outside of your homework, you are only permitted to work on the projects I've set for you. Do you understand?"

Nia nodded her head.

"Good."

There's a thin line between discipline and abuse. I didn't feel like a whooping would suffice. Nia was old enough at the time to understand that what she did was wrong. I wanted to convey the seriousness and danger of her actions, so I talked to her and punished her. I still had the control, and whatever I had to do to reel her in, I was determined to do.

Luckily, Nia wasn't faced with such a hard upbringing as me. For the most part, I kept a roof over her head, food in her belly, clothes on her back, and I was physically present.

I was involved in her academics. I did all of the things my mother didn't, so I'd be damned if I let the streets get ahold of her. Honestly, that was why I didn't want Nia spending her leisure time after school in Brevoort at my sister, Gloria's.

"When I say come straight home, I mean it. Do not — and I repeat, do not — stop at Auntie Glo's house."

"Sometimes I have to use the bathroom after I get off the 46 bus, and you know Auntie's house is closer than home, Ma."

"I don't care, Nia. Hold it until you make it home. If you held it all that long, what's the harm in walking three more blocks? You shouldn't even be taking the 46 bus home because it's not the closest route."

Nia rolled her eyes and sucked her teeth.

"The other bus takes forever to come, and I like riding with my friends on the 46."

"Nia, I don't care. From now on, get your ass on that Q24 bus so you're closer to home. I will be calling your phone at 3:05pm sharp every day."

"Oh, my godddd," Nia said.

I became infuriated. Why was this girl so damn mouthy?

"Talk back to me one more fucking time. You are on punishment! What part of no hanging out don't you understand? You can't be trusted. You out here on chatlines talking to grown-ass men, tryna give up ya little pussy. Bitch, that's my pussy."

Nia stood shyly with her arms folded and a pout on her lips. I walked up to her and stood boldly in her face.

"What the fuck you know about a man?" I asked between a sarcastic chuckle.

She remained silent.

"Quiet now, huh? Nah, I want to hear this. What you know about talking to a man? ANSWER ME!" I demanded.

Tears began to form in Nia's eyes.

"Stop that fucking crying before I give you something to cry about. Now talk to me. Why were you on a chatline talking to older men?"

Fighting back tears, Nia said, "Because they're the only ones that like me, that look at me. The boys my age like all the skinny girls."

"Nia, I don't care how grown you look. You're still a little girl, and any grown man talking to you is a pedophile. And if I find out about it, they're going to jail, and you'll never be off punishment. Try me if you want, little bitch."

Nia held her head down as she proceeded to leave the living room and head back into her room. Before she could get far, I yelled out to her,

"And keep my fucking door open. You don't pay no bills in here to be locking or closing doors."

Now that Nia confirmed that grown men were checking for her, my anxiety grew. The truth of the matter was that I couldn't control everything. I couldn't control who Nia bumped into while on her way to school because I was on my way to work. I couldn't control who she met after school because I was still at work and not set to get off until two hours later, like most parents.

Kids needed to be occupied after school to stay out of trouble. The worst thing, in my opinion, was to allow her to have so much free time after school. Nia had always been naturally smart and inquisitive, so her grades always remained high. I had nothing to worry about when it came to her academics. I just wanted to do my very best to monitor her out-of-school activities. I didn't hang out in the projects, so I didn't want that for my daughter either. I was out getting money in and out of state.

I was known in Brevoort for being fly and selling the hottest designer clothing for half price. Other than business, I was barely in Brevoort because I wasn't raised there. I moved there as a teenager and already had my set of friends on the other side of Bed Stuy. I always felt like the projects were designed to box you in and keep you stagnant. Every project had playgrounds, benches, community centers, and even pools. All of the basic necessities were at arm's length, preventing you from venturing out of your small radius.

While living in the projects was affordable and a stepping-stone for some, it was a way of life for many. There were generations and generations born and raised in the same apartment. When the daughter became grown, when she turns eighteen or had a baby and could get her own welfare budget.

This was what I did not want for Nia, so I reeled her in. I did my best to shelter her, which was why I went with Section 8, versus applying for housing. I didn't care about the benefits of dirt-cheap rent with water and gas included. I would have rather paid near-market rent, which was based on my income, than raise my daughter in the projects. If I had taken an apartment in the projects, I would have had to groom Nia to be equipped to handle the streets.

Although my apartment was just three blocks away, it was in a private building and free of the demons that lurked in high story buildings with thousands of residents. I didn't have to shock Nia with fear. I didn't have to explain what a dope fiend looked like and how to avoid or ignore them at such a young age. I didn't have to worry about her being kidnapped from her building and escorted to the roof to perform sexual acts for a gang of boys. She wasn't ready to handle boys, let alone men. She didn't know her father nearly as well as I knew my Daddy — drug addict or not. She wasn't equipped to deal with the lies, half-truths, and innuendos these men concocted. I wanted to shield my daughter from abuse, confusion, and heartache, and whatever I had to do to achieve that, I was willing to do.

CHAPTER 6

WOMAN

female person who plays a significant role (wife or mistress or girlfriend) in the life of a particular man

Tony and I hadn't known each other for more than two months before he surprised me with tickets to go to Jamaica. I wasn't skeptical. I wasn't afraid. He was so gentle when he asked me to go with him. He didn't make a big deal of it.

We were on our first date in Prospect Park, having a picnic with a few spliffs and beers when he said, "Babes mi go dun to JA. Mi wan yuh fawad wid mi."

He pulled out the tickets and laid them on the sheet we sat on top of on the grass to assert his level of seriousness. I was so excited. Although Pam was born in Barbados, making me of Caribbean descent, I had never been to the Caribbean or anywhere out of the country. This was also the first time a man asked me on a vacation. My ex, Clyde, never took me anywhere.

He didn't even drive or have a passport.

"Wow, Mr. Tony Skank, you really pulling out all your stops for little ole me!" I exclaimed in a whimsical cheer.

"Nuh stops, jus regular tings yuh kno for mi Princess." He picked up my hand and kissed it.

I couldn't lie; I was blown away. I couldn't fake it; I was open. Flashes of a beautiful garden full of roses and lilies sprang in my head as I closed my eyes and fantasized about what it felt like to live in heaven. Being with Tony felt that good. Then, I snapped out of it and opened my eyes. It wasn't a dream. Once I saw that he was serious, I figured that I'd get serious and start asking the important questions.

"You know about my daughter already, but what about you? Just how many kids do you have back in Jamaica?"

He chuckled.

"Mi nuh shamed ov mi pickneys. Mi ah eight in total. One live hea wid mi an di otha dem grown and back home wid dem own pickney. Yuh see!"

A burning sting pierced my heart as he unconsciously bragged about his children and grandkids. I always longed for a big family. Although I had a big family through my father, it didn't compare to having a big family of my own. I was only blessed with Nia. Pam was only blessed with three — me, my sister, Gloria, and my little brother. Pam herself was an only child. I didn't know many people who had more than five kids. Certainly, no one in my family or extended family had more than three children.

"How nice," I said.

Hopefully, he didn't hear the saltiness in my galled response.

Before I could commit to flying out with Tony, I had to make sure Nia was situated. Instead of having Pam or Gloria look after her, I decided to send Nia to her aunt's house in Connecticut. My baby daddy might have abandoned us while in jail, but he tried his best to make up for it in the later years. Nia's aunt, my baby daddy's sister, went out of her way to make sure Nia was included, and that she met her cousins and other siblings. I was truly thankful for that.

On the day of our flight, Tony came to pick me up from my apartment at six am. We flew out of LaGuardia Airport, which was eight minutes away from Rikers Island. Our check-in process was smooth. Tony handled everything with our bags while I curiously studied my surroundings. The airport floors were stark and sparkling white with no stain in sight.

People of every culture lugged suitcases across the room while waving goodbye to relatives. Sadly, this brought flashbacks of the visiting room at Rosie. Waiting in line for TSA and being searched also took me back to the day I got booked. It felt like I was reliving the entire experience — until we got through to the shops and I saw Dunkin Donuts and Popeyes.

The plane was crowded with tired and weary faces. The wheel of my carry-on snagged against every row as I strolled down the narrow aisle behind Tony. Once settled in our seats, Tony placed his hand on my thigh and gave it a gentle and comforting squeeze. As we started to take off, I felt an awful ache in both of my ears. Shortly after, I fell asleep with my head on his chest.

Once we landed into Montego Bay International Airport, our first stop was to the Money Exchange Booth. Tony, wearing a red, mesh, fishnet wife beater with a pair of white and red True Religion shorts, and the latest Jordans with his long dreads sitting on his head wrapped into a beehive, pulled out two wads of cash with at least fifty, hundred-dollar bills.

I stood shyly behind him as he spoke into the intercom on the glass separating him and the teller.

"Gal giv mi dit town rate — this stack in JMD and di next stack in GBP."

The teller hesitated at first then responded.

"Nuh suh cyant give town rate. We hea in di airport. Nuh work."

Tony dug into his back pocket and pulled out three hundred-dollar bills and slid it in the slot.

"Gal, take $150 USD fuh yuh trouble an exchange mi rest. Peace an bless from Jah, Di Most High!"

The teller looked embarrassed and quickly apologized.

"Sure, sure, Rasta. Mi sorry. Mi nuh know. Doh worry 'bout it," she said, pushing the money back in the slot towards Tony.

"No worry, gal. Mi still need mi money exchange fuh mi gal hea. Give she," he said before moving to the side to expose me from hiding comfortably behind him. He stepped to the side and took off his Gucci backpack.

I was thrown for a loop and just stood there frozen, about two to three feet from the counter.

"Joi, gwan git it fuh me in two envelopes." He nodded his head towards the glass counter.

When I looked up at the short, light-skinned teller, she had a nasty look on her face. She rolled her eyes, sucked her teeth, and looked me up and down. She held her head to the side with her lips pursed like a duck while she counted out the cash. Once finished, she placed the envelopes through the slot with a receipt attached.

Confused at her attitude, I sarcastically said, "Thank you. Have a nice day." Appalled by my audacity, she responded lowly, almost whispering,

"Bye, bitch."

I turned around, laughed to myself, and passed Tony the envelopes. He was kneeling on the floor, making space in his bag. He buried both envelopes in his bag, closed it, and stood up. After he put his backpack on, he dug in his back pocket and counted out thirty, one- hundred-dollar U.S. bills and passed it to me as we stood right in front of the teller.

"Hea, princess. Put dat away. Nuh worry — exchange money fuh di villagers. We roll only U.S. money. Yuh suh me." He grabbed my hand firmly as we walked out of the airport to be greeted by an SUV that already had our luggage neatly packed inside.

Once settled inside of the car, I turned to Tony and asked, "What the fuck was her problem?"

Tony cupped my chin with his hand, leaned closer to my face, and said, "If yuh cyan see how yuh beauty can cause such jealousy, yuh just might be blind, gal."

I instantly started blushing, and he kissed me slowly and passionately. Our kiss seemed endless, like the ocean. We didn't even mind that the AC was not on.

The driver jumped in the car, booted up the engine, and the cold breeze cooled us down. He rolled down his window and passed Tony three tightly rolled spliffs.

"Rasta man, wea yuh wan mi fuh carry yuh an yuh Queen off tuh?"

Tony unlocked his lips from mine, grabbed my thigh, and excitedly yelled,

"Ochi Town, mon. DRIVER DOH STOP AT ALLLLLLLLLLLLLLL."

I laughed hysterically and rested my head on his chest as he lit his spliff, and we rode into paradise.

* * *

JAMAICA WAS BEAUTIFUL AND WARM. It was early August, and the heat was a bit intense. It felt so good to momentarily escape the drama back home and bury the past with Clyde. I felt myself changing and growing as soon as I stepped foot off the plane. For the first time in my life, I felt like I was in a mature, healthy, adult relationship.

There was a lot of love awaiting Tony when we got to Ocho Rios, which he calls Ochi Town. All seven of his kids were excited to see him. The oldest was twenty-eight and the youngest was twelve — five boys and two girls. Two of his sons were about three to four years younger than me.

His oldest daughter was my buddy while Tony ran around the island to visit relatives and friends. She was nineteen and stark tall just like her daddy. West Indians have an interesting concept of color. Tony told me that Simone was light-skinned. In actuality, she was a chocolate, mocha hue. I guess in comparison to Tony; she was of lighter skin. I'm a brown-skinned girl and never felt ashamed of my color. I'd never even desired to be light-skinned like most brown girls I grew up with.

I sure looked beautiful in my bathing suit and short haircut climbing the falls at Dunn's River. I felt refreshed, relaxed, and resurrected from the pits of complacency being with Tony. He was the first man to expose me to the Caribbean.

Despite my grandmother being born and owning land there, I never felt connected to my West Indian roots until I met Tony. Meeting his family just intensified my new fondness of the Caribbean. I instantly felt a part of his family, and it felt so good to be accepted.

We had a time drinking, laughing, and partying. All of Tony's sons were over six feet, lean, and strong. They stood with bowlegs just like Tony. I found this so appealing. Everywhere we went, I was protected. They were my personal bodyguards.

"Gal, yuh nuh talk. Cyan let no one hear yuh so," Tony's oldest son warned while looking back at me from the driver's seat of the car.

We were heading to Kingston for a day of sightseeing and shopping.

"Once they hear that American accent, gal, you's a dead woman. All they see is money," Tony warned, adding his two cents. I took heed to his advice and remained quiet as a church mouse.

Kingston looked exactly like Flatbush Junction in Brooklyn — full of color and street hustlers selling CDs, clothes, and food. The women dressed just like us. They wore their hair like us, too. The only difference we shared was our accents.

While walking around one of the markets, I lost sight of Tony — only his tallest son was around at that moment. The other two must have disappeared with Tony. Unlike the other brothers, he didn't talk much. Apprehension was written all over his posture.

"Where yuh fadda?" I asked, forcing a Jamaican accent.

He didn't respond. He just stood frozen and ignored my question. His body looked very uncomfortable as if he felt out of place. I was annoyed and confused and instantly diagnosed him with a strange personality disorder. I shrugged it off with a laugh and turned around. I spotted Tony directly in my view. He wasn't alone, but his two sons weren't with him.

He stood face to face with a big woman who wore a long, denim skirt and ankle-length dreadlocks. Her hair was so heavy, it weighed her neck down, which made her look much shorter than she actually was. She wore bright red, yellow, and green bangles and a hair scarf tied around her head. Although she tried, her colorful appearance couldn't drown out the desperation and gloom on her face. The sight of her was dreadful.

WHILE SHE SPOKE TO TONY, his body language displayed clear disinterest. I continued to watch the exchange from afar. The two of them were completely lost in the moment and enthralled with emotional tension that neither he nor she saw me openly gawking at them – not even thirty feet away. To me and Tony's surprise, she grabbed him by the hand and hugged him. He engaged yet looked highly uncomfortable.

"Okay. Okay, woman. Cool it," Tony said while tearing her hands off of him.

"Bubs. Doh act so so wid me," she responded.

Tony turned around and walked directly toward me as if he knew I was standing there all along. He looked me in my eyes, and our magnetic exchange confirmed that we both witnessed a woman in desperation.

"Come on, babes," he said while grabbing me by the hand as we left the market. I was quiet for what felt like an eternity. It wasn't until we got in the car that I realized his sons were not with us. *They must have been back at the market where we left them,* I thought.

"Who was that woman you were talking to, Tone?"

Without any hesitation at all, he replied, "That's my wife."

CHAPTER 7

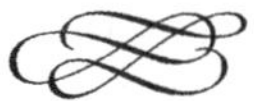

THE FUN IN IT

enjoyment, amusement, or pleasure

For the remainder of the trip, I was unfazed. I pushed it out of my mind and continued to enjoy myself. There was no way I would allow that news to ruin my first trip overseas.

I continued to have fun, carelessly forgetting about my past and intentionally not thinking about the future. I just decided to live in the moment. I was thirty-one, healthy, happy, employed, and currently on vacation! I allowed nothing to worry me. Not even the crappy weather towards the end of the trip could move me from the complete feeling of joy.

The tropical storms of hurricane season hit us hard, and it rained for four days consistently. Snuggling under the covers watching the rainfall with Tony was just perfect for me. His long arms draped around my entire body as he held me close. I soaked in the manly musk he smelled of, brushing my face against the soft bristle of his hair.

His scent was light and earthy. These days, we spent time

completely alone without any kids or relatives. The level of peace I experienced in Tony's presence made me forget all about his wife. No drama, no scene, and no strife. How was it that doing something so wrong felt so right and so divinely healthy? Clyde was a fully single man, yet worry, fear, and disharmony always lingered around us.

Nothing at this moment worried me. Not even Nia. I completely trusted my judgment. I trusted myself, my judgment of Tony's character, and my decision to let Nia stay with her aunt in Connecticut while I enjoyed my getaway.

Nia needed to spend the summer getting to know her cousins. I was proud of myself for not obsessing about what she was doing, every moment of the day. I spoke with her twice, and she sounded like she was having a blast. Two weeks in bliss went by fast. Because the last few days were rainy, Tony extended our stay an additional week. Thank God I rarely traveled and had enough vacation days to take off from work.

After Nia spent the first two weeks in Connecticut, she stayed the remaining week at Pam's house. Although I knew drug-addicted Pam, Nia never witnessed Pam as a fiend. She adored her grandmother just as I wanted.

Nia wasn't privy to any of Pam's past, and I never talked about my momma's business in front of my child. I never spoke ill of Pam around Nia, and I wasn't going to allow it from anyone. It was important to me that Nia respected her grandmother regardless of any stigma or Pam's choices. Nia was a child, and children needed to stay in a child's place.

Since Pam was clean, she was a great influence on Nia. She taught Nia how to speak eloquently and expand her vocabulary. The drugs never stopped Pam from being a lady at all times.

She rarely wore jeans. She was always dressed in a skirt or slacks. Her esteem always remained high. Pam instilled the importance of loving yourself and working with what you had to make yourself happy. High or sober, Pam maintained her style and her vigor. These were traits I wanted Nia to embrace.

With vacation over, I was happy to get back home to my baby girl and hear all about her summer. The night Tony and I flew back in, it was hot and humid – mid August. LaGuardia Airport was mildly crowded with travelers voyaging from everywhere afar. We lugged four heavy suitcases through the crowd, three of Tony's and one belonged to me. He brought back tons of souvenirs, family portraits, and trinkets from his childhood home.

Dashing down the Brooklyn-Queens Expressway, I looked out of the window into a sky of darkness. This time, I counted twelve small shining stars and let their twinkle light up my heart. I hadn't felt this happy in a very long time.

Tony dropped me off at Pam's new apartment. Since she was released from the program, she refused to return to the projects. Besides the fact that Gloria was now occupying the apartment, Pam was shielding herself from the demons and toxic, addicting memories of comfort she created there. So, instead, she rented out a small, one-bedroom apartment on Tompkins Avenue. She went from apartment 4D in the projects to 4A on a quiet, residential block in Bed Stuy. Unfortunately, she didn't have an elevator, so I had to walk up four flights of stairs. Tony carried my suitcase up for me.

"Hey, Ma," I panted excitedly after she opened the door. I leaned in for a kiss, and she accepted it.

"Hey, Ms. Thing. How was your trip?" she asked before she recognized Tony with a huge suitcase in his hand.

"Hello, Mister," she said, directing her speech to Tony.

"Yes, yes. Goodnight, Ms. Pam. How are you?" Tony asked as he blanketed his accent with a more American tone.

"I'm doing good. It's nice to see you," she replied.

Tony neatly placed my suitcase against the wall. He walked over to me, pulled me closer, and kissed my neck. "I'm gonna head out, babes. I'll see you soon," he said before closing the door behind him.

I walked into the apartment, and Nia was sitting on Pam's green futon, wearing a long T-Shirt, a dismayed face, and an uneasy composure.

"Hey, baby. I got you some gifts from Jamaica. Go over there and get my suitcase," I said, leaning in to kiss her forehead. I felt a sense of malaise from Nia, and I was confused. As Nia got up to walk towards the suitcase, Pam came out of her bedroom and plopped herself right next to me on the couch.

"Come here, baby girl," Pam said, motioning Nia over. Nia held her head down and walked over to us.

"Listen, Joi. Nia has something to share with you. I want you to prepare yourself."

Nia came to the couch and sat beside Pam, who was in between us, completely hiding Nia's face and body. Pam grabbed my hand with her left and Nia's hand with her right. She turned her body to Nia and said, "It's okay, baby girl. You can tell her."

Nia's face was full of fluster, fear, and worry. She stayed quiet for a moment and then took a deep breath.

"I had sex, Mommy."

CHAPTER 8

INCEPTION

The ability to influence people in a positive or negative manner.

"How long did you know about this, Ma?" I asked, turning to Pam.

"About three weeks — while you were in Jamaica."

My heart sank as defeat began to settle in. While I was in Jamaica having the time of my life, my adolescent daughter was running wild and fucking. My biggest nightmare. I was not prepared to come home and deal with this. I had tons of gifts for Nia, as well as a host of stories to share with her. I wanted her to sit on my lap while I showed her pictures from my Sony digital camera of Dunn's River Falls and James Bond Beach.

Instead, I was forced to reprimand, correct, and scold her. No amount of logic or rationale could excuse my disappointment and make me feel better. A twelve-year-old should not be having sex — not in America, Brazil, or Jamaica.

But mine was. Nia lost her virginity even before I did. I didn't have sex for the first time until I was sixteen with my steady boyfriend.

Pam knew him and welcomed him over to the house as long as he had some money or crack for her. His grandmother knew exactly who I was. There was no way Nia had a boyfriend and I didn't know about it. So, who the hell did she have sex with? I sat quiet for what seemed like an eternity until I turned to Nia with tears in my eyes.

"Who was it?" I asked disappointedly.

Nia remained silent with her head down. Shame overtook her as she remained mute.

"Nia, talk to your mother. Tell her, she's right here listening."

What was intended to translate as a demand showed up as Pam pleading for Nia to open up to me, her mother. Pam stroked Nia's thigh and said, "C'mon, baby girl, you got this."

"Ma… Mom…meee… I'm so sorry," was all Nia managed to finally get it out.

"Just answer the damn question, Nia! WHO DID YOU HAVE SEX WITH?"

"You don't know him."

"So, who the fuck is he and how do you know him?" I screamed so loud that white suds foamed near the corners of my mouth.

"How old is this nigga? Where did you meet him? Your aunt's house?

Nia remained quiet and continued to hang her head low.

"You hear me talking to you, little bitch? Oh, so you really think you grown. Gimme your aunt's number. I'm gon' have a talk with her because I want to know how the hell I send my daughter to Connecticut a virgin, and she comes back turned out."

I grabbed Nia forcefully by the neck 'til her face was so close to my mouth that I nearly slobbered on her cheek. I stared her dead in the eyes as I said,

"I'm giving you one final chance to tell me the truth before I beat it out of you. There ain't nobody to save you, and your grandmother can't do a damn thing either."

* * *

THE CONVERSATION with Nia's aunt didn't go well. This was the first time I'd allowed my daughter to visit her. Worst part of it all was that Nia's aunt had no idea what happened. Apparently, she had a house full of teenagers, yet no answers. Although I was upset, I knew that there was nothing she could have done to prevent it. However, I wanted her to hear and feel my grief. Her daughter is the same age as Nia. It shouldn't have been hard for her to empathize with my pain and confusion.

WHILE I WAS TRYING to reprimand and protect Nia, Pam was encouraging preteen sex by giving my daughter condoms. I found them in her school bag. I couldn't help myself from checking her things, snooping through her room, and monitoring her phone calls and text messages. I became obsessed. I wanted to know who she was talking to, who her friends were, what boys she liked, and who liked her.

My anxiety only got worse after seeing the condoms, so I approached her angrily.

"So, since you had sex once, now you need condoms with you at all times? Who you plan on fucking now, you little slut?"

"Grandma Pam gave them to me, Mommy. I told her I didn't need them. I don't want to have sex anymore," she replied back sweetly.

Her tone gave me nostalgia. It took me back to the days when she was an innocent, cute, light-skinned baby with a shining forthrightness that always peeked through.

I'll never forget the time she reprimanded me for talking to her harshly at the age of five. Whatever I said to her disrupted her soul. Barely reaching three feet tall, she looked at me and said shyly, "That's not how you talk to a little girl." I laughed to myself thinking, "this little girl is a piece of work, but she's right."

I don't know how much I believed her, but I was happy to hear her disinterest in sex. Sex is for grown folks. It comes with too many consequences, conflicting emotions, and possibilities of abuse for me to condone my adolescent daughter having consistent, casual sex. I wouldn't allow it. I needed Pam to know it also. What the hell was she thinking when she gave Nia condoms? I was determined to find out.

Immediately after work the very next day, I ran to Pam's apartment on Tompkins Avenue. She didn't even expect me. Once buzzed in, I rushed up her awfully loud squeaky stairs. Normally, I was out of breath, huffing and puffing. But this day, my adrenaline was pumping. I needed answers. I knocked on her door twice before she answered.

"Hey, Sista Suki, what's going on?" she probed with suspense.

She wore a long, cream, lace robe that draped her body perfectly. Her dark, chocolate skin radiated in it. I stormed in and shut the door behind me. It made a loud creaking sound as I slowly walked into her apartment, hands on my hips and a pout on my lip. I cut my eyes at her sharply and turned my mouth up in disgust. Her apartment was quiet in sound but strong in scent. I was instantly hit with an overpowering combination of roses and moth balls.

"What were you thinking giving my daughter condoms?"

Pam paused and sat down on her green, leather couch before answering. She folded her arms and crossed her legs.

"Joi, Nia is having sex. I just want her to be safe."

"Nia is NOT having sex. Also, it's not YOUR PLACE to give her condoms. What's next? Birth control? Nia is my daughter, and she's not walking around with condoms like a grown ass woman."

Pam chuckled as she unfolded her legs and arms. She sat up straight, almost erect-like.

"Listen, your daughter is out here fucking, and you don't even know with whom. So yes, the cunt needs to walk around with condoms," she said firmly before standing up and heading to her room.

"This bitch wanna come in my house and tell me about her daughter this and her daughter that, please! Your daughter came to me with her secret, and I made her tell you. GET THE FUCK OUT OF MY HOUSE, JOI! NOW!"

* * *

I WAS JUST SOAKING in bliss in Jamaica. To be bombarded with Nia's sexscapade and to face the fact that my newfound love was a married man was too much to process. I still had tons of questions, and answers were required.

FROM TONY I wanted to know the full story. Is he a serial cheater? Is he unhappy in his marriage and wanted out or does he just wanna have his cake and eat it too? Does she live at home with him, or does she live in Jamaica? For me, that was the most crucial question, and it ultimately would determine my next course of action.

Thinking back to the day at the market when I saw his wife, Tony had been disinterested in her conversation and presence. She was practically throwing herself at him. It was honestly a miserable sight to see. Was it all just an act? Tony knew I was somewhere not too far away watching him. Or, was he really in a loveless marriage?

Should the circumstances matter? Or is dating a married man completely off limits? This was a morality check for myself, and I didn't even have the answers. I knew it was just too good to be true but all the more it felt amazing. Despite the terrifying mystery that awaited, *I was intrigued.* I genuinely wanted to know his side of the story. I wasn't even angry with him. I just wanted a peek into his world.

I let about three weeks pass before I saw him again. I didn't exactly ignore his calls; I just kept them very brief. He'd call and I would rush him off the phone in a couple of minutes. The first time he asked to see me, I told him that Nia had an asthma attack, and I was stuck home caring for her. The second time, I told him that I would be out of town visiting my father in Virginia. After that, I replied, "I'll let you know." I never addressed him about his wife on the phone. To be frank, I was still deciding how I felt about it and if I should even care. My rationale was that his marriage only mattered if I planned to take him seriously, and I didn't.

Before I could make the official decision that I didn't mind continuing our relationship, he showed up to my apartment. It was a Sunday evening when I heard my doorbell ring. Nia was sitting on a comforter between my legs as I braided her hair for school.

"Nia, go see who that is at the door," I said.

Nia, who hadn't exactly outgrown her baby fat, struggled to stand up and walk over to the buzzer on the wall.

"Who is it?"

A raspy voice purred through the intercom and said, "Tony Skank looking for sweet Joi."

I instantly felt butterflies in my stomach.

He came looking for me. Wow. I was shocked. He had yet to see the inside of my apartment or known that I lived on the fourth floor, specifically 4A. He had only dropped me off outside after a few date nights. Hmm. Had he bugged my neighbors, ringing their bell mistakenly before he found me?

"Nia, I got it. Come sit down."

I hurried over to the intercom and pressed the talk button. I spoke low but clearly.

"You're real bold coming here, Mr. Tony Skank. Gimme a minute. I'm coming down," I said.

I slipped into my house shoes, threw on a sweater, and rushed down the stairs. I saw his tall stature through the window as I approached the top of the last flight. As I decreased my speed to a slow step, inches away from him in the flesh, I could see he was leaning his back on the gate and wearing a green, fishnet tank and black jean shorts. Sporting his usual messy beehive, his dreadlocks looked incredibly heavy to the eyes, yet he stood high and unbothered. I opened the door, and his eyes lit up.

"Babes, wea yu? I been tryna see yuh from long time nuh. Doh tell me yuh avoiding me," he said as he grabbed me by the wrists.

Do I keep it real about how I feel or do I pretend to not care?

Pam always taught me to never tell a man my real thoughts. They never cared anyway. They only cared about your actions. How you feel is irrelevant and even inconceivable to them.

I just couldn't help it.

"To be honest, I don't know what situation you got going on, but I'm falling back from you."

"Wah situation, gal?" he asked, dumbfounded. He was dead serious, and his genuine curiosity amused, annoyed, and angered me simultaneously.

I took a sigh and a step back before folding my arms under my chest.

Niggas can be so damn ignorant.

"Your wife!" I responded as I raised my eyebrows, rolled my eyes, and cracked a sarcastic smile.

Tony sucked his teeth loud, fast, and with a sharpness that rendered my response bullshit. He pulled me closer and looked me in the eyes before saying,

"Marcia. She mi son mudda and mi legal wife, but me and she doy haf nuttin gwan. Trust mi, babygirl. She bring mi hea to di U.S.."

I shrugged away from him, hitting him in the side with my folded elbow.

"Do y'all live together?

"No, not really."

"What does that mean?"

"We live inna same house, yes, suh buh wea nuh together more so, how yuh say? Roommates. Wea like roommates. Mi can sleep out nights if mi like."

"I don't know what to believe. All I know is I ain't really feeling you right now."

He grabbed me again, this time holding me tightly and rocking me by the waist.

"It okay if yuh nuh feel mi rite now. Mi ah give yuh some time gal," he said in between chuckles, "but yuhs gon' feel mi soon cuz mi already feelin' yuh."

I couldn't help but laugh with him. He was so charming and lighthearted. Being in his arms again reminded me of how free I felt with him.

"Listen, babes, yuh haf nuttin' at all fuh worry 'bout. Mi want yuh. Mi ah come all dis way fuh invite yuh out to dinner wid mi next week.

Mi nuh tek no fuh answa. Mi get tired ah calling yuh. Cum fuh dinner wid me. Mi'll tell yuh everyting 'bout mi an' Marcia.

I rolled my eyes, tilted my head to the side, and let out a big sigh.

"Mi nuh tek no fuh answer," he said, repeating himself.

"What'chu gon' do? Kidnap me?"

We both looked at each other and busted out laughing.

"Gal, yuh funny. But forreal, babes. Cum on," he said, pleading.

"Alright, alright. Call me tomorrow. Let me sleep on it."

"Okay, Princess, yuh got it. Mi ah call yuh." Before I could back away, Tony planted a kiss on my forehead. I chuckled and released from his embrace and turned around to open the front door. He began to walk away. Before I shut the door, I heard him yell out,

"Joi! Mek sure yuh answer yuh phone."

CHAPTER 9

SALTY

annoyed or upset when something is unreasonable.

I slept on it. He called. I answered. And we met for lunch the week after. He picked me up at my apartment in a different SUV and not his usual, white Lincoln Navigator. This time, he arrived in a plush, cream Cadillac Escalade truck. It was a comfortable afternoon nearing the end of summer. The chilly September breeze confirmed that fall was right around the corner. I wore a white skirt, fuchsia and beige wedge sandals, a white blouse, and a pink, long, silk cardigan. Classy and sophisticated.

I never dressed like this with Clyde. I normally wore hip hop gear — the latest sneakers, Rocawear jeans, or a Baby Phat sweatsuit. Being with Tony made me feel like a woman and made me want to act like a lady. I could already tell that he was a different type of man than Clyde was.

Back in Pam's day, she messed with a lot of white men. She always told me, "White men like their women to behave and look like ladies.

Always wear heels, lipstick, and your best perfume. Smile a lot, laugh at their jokes, and don't curse."

Although Tony wasn't a white man or a single man, I felt the need to switch up my style and impress him by putting my best foot forward. In all of the eleven years Clyde and I had been together, I never got dressed with him in mind. I never thought to myself, *what would my man like to see me in?* In my mind, Clyde should have been happy with just being in my presence and having the privilege to have a young, sexy PYT on his arm. With Tony, it was different. I felt like he was a prize, and I wanted to do everything in my power to win him over.

I wanted him to find me attractive. I wanted to learn more about his culture and upbringing. I wanted to be introduced to new things. I wanted to have conversations that didn't involve hooking or crooking. I wanted a breath of fresh air, and since I met Tony, he'd shown me that. Meeting for lunch was no different.

We rode to a quiet neighborhood in Queens, where there were so many Indian looking people. Some looked blacker than others. Once we got into the quaint restaurant, I heard their accents, and they sounded just like Jamaicans. I was confused. They didn't look mixed or what we grew up saying, "Coolie. The "Coolie" people I knew had black features with good hair that was normally silky and curly just like my natural hair that I hated. Considering that my Dad's side of the family had Blackfoot Indian roots, I was familiar with the variety of skin tones and hair textures, But these people truly looked Indian from their features, not just the hair. However, their accent threw it off.

"What's good to eat here, babe? How're their oxtails?" I turned and asked Tony as he stood tall and looked straight at the menu. Meanwhile, my short self had to look up.

"No oxtails here, babes. Yuh forget mi ah rasta? Tis Ital spot. All vegetarian food and products."

"Vegetarian? As in no meat? I ain't up for this at all," I complained and immediately sucked my teeth and folded my arms.

"Doh worry yaself gal. Yuh gwan like it. Lemme order fuh yuh.

I sure fucking hope so, was all I could think to myself.

To my surprise, the food was tasty and flavorful. Tony ordered lo mein, a veggie fish patty, and vegan chicken on a stick.

"How do they get the food to taste so good if it's not real meat?" I asked dumbfounded.

"It mek outta soy. Dem engineer it so it cyan taste like di real ting. Much healthier fuh yuh than red meat." he responded.

I was warming up to his accent. No longer was it difficult to understand him and make out what he meant.

He shoved a forkful of lo mein in his mouth. He sucked up the entire half of his noodle and leaned over to kiss me. I grabbed the end of the noodle and sucked it up until our lips met, and we exchanged a deep, passionate kiss. It was exhilarating. I wanted more.

Tony's coolness definitely intrigued me. His demeanor was so gentle, and his poise was so naturally confident. He seemed very secure in his manhood, not having to force his way or overexert himself. He was calm and radiated a sense of pure patience, making it easy for me to be comfortable and trust him.

Believe it or not, it was easy to forget that he was married, but I couldn't get wrapped up in a fantasy. I was not a young, inexperienced teenager so why was I feeling butterflies in my belly? This was a married man. Where was this really gonna go? I guess I was here to find out.

Tony placed his hand over my hand before saying,

"Listen, Joi, mi nuh try tuh mix yuh up in all mi dealings, but mi gwan tawk tuh yuh plain. Mi nuh happy fuh long time, since mi been here in America. Mi nuh marry for love. Mi marry fuh opportunity, and most importantly, fuh watch out fuh my son. Listen ,Joi, mi wife is wicked. Tree months afta she give birth to mi bwoy bwoy, she left him, she own pickney with she neighbor and flee to America. As soon mi find out, mi gwan dung fuh git mi bwoy from di neighbor and raised he in Jamaica fuh seven years. Mi beg she fuh just file and send fuh de bwoy. She say nuh- dat if he wah cum – she spect mi fuh cum too and di only way fuh cum to America wid — we have fuh wed and git married."

All I could muster up to say was "Uh huh. Isn't that what they all say? So, if your wife brought you up here, why was she in Jamaica with us?"

"Eveybody go dung Jamaica round det time of August fuh we Independence Day. Big big celebration gal."

"Uh hmm," was all I could muster up.

"Joi, listen to me — every woman mi been wid mi ah use mi head. Tis time, mi ah use mi heart. So, either it'll be wid you or someone else, but nuh Marcia."

I had to respect the man's honesty. Either he was gonna cheat with me or someone else, but either way, his wife was not an option.

POST JAMAICA BLISS and being in la la land had to come to an end. As Pam always said, "All that other shit is secondary. You're a mother first." I had been back in the states for about two weeks and still couldn't get an immediate appointment at the clinic to take Nia to see the GYN. I still had an ounce of hope left that miraculously, the doctor would find Nia's hymen still intact and that she didn't have sex. I was almost certain that wasn't the case, but a little bit of hope couldn't hurt, right?

After calling about six clinics, I was finally able to secure a date for three weeks out at a new facility. Once that was done, I began to sort through the week's mail, trying my best to avoid bills, which was nearly impossible. While tossing envelopes addressed from CableVision and T-Mobile to the back of the pile, a 4x6 postcard fell out of the pile.

It was a white card with a picture of a Panda on it. No text, but the addressed name read *Nia Holloway*. There was no return address.

What the hell is this? I thought. I know Nia wasn't involved in any school clubs, so I wanted to know who this postcard was from. When Nia arrived home, I called her.

"Nia, come here," I shouted from the living room. Within thirty seconds, she appeared.

"Yes, ma?"

"Look here, I set up an appointment for you at the GYN." She looked puzzled.

"What's that?"

"The pussy doctor. You be all up in grown folks' conversations, especially mine. I know you've heard the word GYN before."

Nia held her head down, twiddled her thumbs, and didn't say anything. I was still angry at her. I was even angrier at myself because I wasn't there to rescue her, to guide her, and talk to her.

"Last thing, Nia, what's this and where's it from?" I asked while holding up the postcard in my hand.

"Mommy, I have something to tell you," Nia said shyly in a soft tone.

"What now?" I scolded.

"After I had sex, Grandma Pam asked Auntie Glo to take me to the doctor. They found out that I had gonorrhea, but they treated it. That's the postcard from the doctor. They said they would send for me to come back."

I was crushed. Everything happened so fast. I was only gone a few weeks, and my baby girl was out here looseballing. What hurt the most was that I wasn't there to protect her, guide her or be there. Yeah, it took a village to raise a child, but lately, it didn't seem like I was a part of that village.

CHAPTER 10

GHETTO FABULOUS

denoting or exemplifying an ostentatious or flamboyant lifestyle or style of clothing of a type associated with the hip-hop subculture.

Some people loved their sisters. Some wished they had sisters. My relationship with my sister was never an easy one. We were so close in age; you'd think we'd be best friends. Deep down in my heart, I knew Gloria loved me, but I was almost certain she didn't like me. Despite how much she was doted on by my grandfather, she was always jealous that I, as the oldest, was smarter and my Daddy's favorite.

Unlike my grandfather, my daddy never displayed favoritism. Tall and solid, my grandfather, who only came around to brag about his latest voyage across Europe and how great Swiss chocolate tasted, was a stoic and militant man with a permanent stiff upper lip. Out of all the times I saw him, he only wore black. He had a brute countenance and a short and direct disposition. He had very little patience or tolerance for uncertainty or stupidity, and he always made sure to remind you how much more he knew than you.

One year, he came to visit for Christmas. I was about twelve years old. My sister had just turned ten on September eleventh, and my brother was not even one. He walked into our apartment with his head high and almost through the ceiling.

"Hey, babe," he said to my mother and nudged her in the side.

"Hey, daddy."

"Where are those kids?"

"Girls! Your grandfather is here to see you," yelled Pam.

Joyful as can be, I ran out of my room briskly, just knowing he was awaiting me in the living room. My photographic memory of his Long Island dock, which stored over twelve big and beautiful boats, flashed in my mind. Having never seen them in person, I vicariously lived through the pictures Pam showed us.

Twelve-year-old me gleamed at him with a big Kool-Aid smile, not prepared to be crushed by what he would say next.

"Not you, not you, the pretty one. Where's the pretty one?" he hissed as he shooed me away with the back of his hand.

As soon as Gloria came running out of the door towards him, his eyes beamed with light.

"Yes, yes, here comes the beauty queen. Come sit on Grandpa's lap. I have something for you."

From that day on, I never cared for my grandfather, and at that very instant, I learned my place with Gloria. Although Daddy would never say such a thing, I knew my grandfather's words were what everyone, including Pam and Daddy, really thought.

Although Gloria was the "pretty one", the "good girl", and my grandfather's favorite, it was never enough for her. She wanted all the attention and all the praise I got for being smarter, stronger, older, and my Daddy's favorite.

Even to this day, Daddy and I have a tight relationship. We talk as often as Pam and I talk even though he's out of the state. The difference between Gloria and I was that I didn't shame my parents for their short comings. I still loved my father despite how many times I had to pay his debts at the local craps spot or pick him up at the bar after he blacked out drinking. My love ran deep for my Daddy because he was there. Drugs, alcohol, or women never stopped him from showing up for us. Wherever he was, even if it was at one of his many girlfriend's houses, we were welcomed.

As I got older, Daddy also confided in and relied on me more, and Glo hated this. She hated that although I was in the streets at a young age while she was in school, our father didn't scold me — he schooled me.

I could hear his voice now.

"Joi, if this boosting shit ain't working, you gotta switch the game. Find a new hustle, baby. If you gon' be in the streets, it's always important to have one foot in and one foot out. You was always smart, so go back to school."

Truthfully, Glo watched me struggle, get arrested several times as a teenager, have Nia in prison, and still manage to get back up, go to school, and keep pushing.

Deep down, I knew her hate for me was rooted in admiration, while her love was displayed in volatile protection. Glo may have talked about me like a dog, but she'd knocked out anybody who spoke ill of me or posed a threat to my safety.

For the most part, Pam raised us to stick together, and we never fell short on that. I was just hoping that Glo's loyalty lied with me over Nia. Before becoming erratic, I decided to give Glo the benefit of the doubt. Maybe she really did plan on telling me but hadn't gotten around to it. Well, I refused to wait any longer, so I made a visit to Brevoort — the apartment Pam raised us in after divorcing my father.

Since Glo took over the apartment, I barely visited unless it was a holiday. Holidays were the only times the apartment would be filled with jovial vibes. Any other time, it was dark and dreary. It didn't help that Glo didn't jazz up the place or even get new furniture. She kept the same green, plastic chairs Daddy bought fifteen years ago.

As I approached the building's front door, the stale stench hit my nostrils immediately. This same smell seeped into the apartment and never left. The hallway light was dim, making it hard to see. I pressed the elevator button and waited patiently. After a few seconds it arrived, and the door opened quickly. Luckily, I looked down before walking in. I was able to avoid stepping in a puddle of urine. I made sure to step over carefully on my way out.

Once on the floor, I walked to the door and knocked. In the next second, I heard a grouchy "who is it?" from behind the door.

"It's Joi, your sister."

She looked through the peephole and began unlocking the three, heavy padlocks she had installed on the door after the police kicked it in a few years back.

She slightly opened the door to where I could only see the shadow of the doorknob.

"You got company with you, sister?"

"Nah, Glo, I'm alone."

"Okay. Okay," she said before opening the door to reveal her standing there, topless with a G-string on.

I scurried past her tall frame and cherry nipples through the dim walkway into the living room, where there was a tad bit more sunlight. Glo never had much breasts. She took after Pam. Small breasts, flat stomach, wide thighs, hourglass frame, and plump booty. I was shorter than her. I had Double D watermelon breasts and some pudge in the belly, but a cute, decent frame.

Her son was sitting on a stool, game controller in hand, with his eyes glued to the TV.

"Hi, Auntie," he said without even turning to me.

"Hey, baby," I responded.

The apartment reeked of a built-up desolate odor. Glo wasn't dirty. She didn't keep a filthy house, but the small apartment locked in years of crack and weed smoke from Pam and burnt oil pots and an overlay of ammonia. The ammonia never successfully masked the aroma of the crack cocaine, but Glo used it faithfully. That's one thing Pam taught us that she upheld. As ghetto fabulous as she was, she still got on her hands and knees and scrubbed the floor with ammonia.

Nearly naked, titties bouncing and pussy popping through her thong, Glo stepped in front of the TV her son was watching.

"Fly Guy, it's time for a break. Gimme the game," she said with her hand out in front of him.

"Pssttt." He sucked his teeth loudly.

"But Ma. Why?"

"Cus me and your Aunt 'bouta talk grown folks' business."

Without thinking, he passed her the controller and rushed to the back, where he took over the room me and Gloria grew up in.

"What's going on, sister?" she inquired as she sat down on the couch with a magazine full of crushed up weed on it.

"When was you gonna tell me you took my daughter to the GYN?"

"I didn't plan on it. How you find out anyway?"

"Even though she contracted a fucking STD, you had no plans of telling me?"

"I had no idea her little fresh ass got no STD. I just went with her to the doctor to get seen. She got her results herself. Doctor made me step outside the room when she was seen anyway. They giving these hot ass girls all these rights to give up they little pussy." She belted out an obnoxious laugh as she laughed.

"Either way, please fucking inform me before you take my daughter anywhere — especially for something like this."

"If she was my daughter, her fresh ass wouldn't be fucking. You island hopping while your hot ass daughter is out here fucking older boys and catching STDs. Apparently, she didn't feel comfortable coming to you, so she came to me. It is what it is."

"Yeah, who better to relate to when it comes to STDs than you?"

I picked up my keys and headed for the door. She hurried in front of me and opened it. I walked a few steps to the elevator, and she followed me out, screaming for the entire building to hear.

"Fuck you and your slut ass daughter. You and her ass both dead to me. Get the fuck out, bitch!"

The elevator didn't come fast enough, so I headed for the stairs. If me and my seed were dead to her, then she was dead to me.

CHAPTER 11

ANSWERS

a thing said, written, or done to deal with or as a reaction to a question, statement, or situation.

I rushed back home immediately. Nia and I were going to get to the bottom of it all. She wasn't my little girl no more; she was baby girl now, and since she wanted to be a big woman, we were gon' talk about this. Truth be told, I was never jealous of the relationship that Nia and Gloria had. It wasn't until Nia told me Glo took her to the GYN that I felt jealousy and disdain towards Glo. Why would Glo, as the adult, think it was appropriate to keep a secret like this from me? So, not only did Nia lose her virginity, but she also contracted an STD. How fucking typical?

Annoyed, I slammed the door shut. The loud slam knocked the picture frame holding Nia's Pre-K photo, on the floor. The glass shattered.

I'll get to that later.

I stormed into Nia's room, where she sat on top of the black and white floor tiles with her back pressed against her wood bed frame with a book in her hand. The TV was on but with the volume very low.

"Put that book down, girl, let me talk to you!" I shouted.

Nia closed the book slowly, raised her eyebrow, and sat it beside her.

"Yes," she said annoyed.

"Listen, this not gon' work between us if we don't have no trust. I am your mother. Not Gloria or Pam. Do you understand me?

She sat on the floor with her arms folded and her knees to her chin with a blank expression on her face.

"You're getting older. If I can't trust that you're gonna be where you say you are, you won't be able to hang out after school, have a job, or participate in after school programs. I am your mother, and I should know where you are at all times. You violated my trust and hurt me by going to everyone else but me. I am the one here for you, taking care of you, providing for you, not your aunt or your grandmother. You are lucky to have a mother who cares as much as I do."

"Mommy, I was scared to tell you. I was scared you would be mad at me. I don't care if Auntie or Grandma Pam get mad. I care if you do."

"If you care so much about me getting mad at you, stay in a child's place. You are a child. Sex is for adults. You are not allowed to have a boyfriend, and you must come home directly after school every day until you gain back my trust. One thing you must learn in life, chicken head, is that trust is not given — it's earned — and when it's lost, it's a hard thing to get back. Your actions have shown me that you can't be trusted."

"Mommy, I'm sorry I disappointed you. I was just scared to tell you."

I truly thanked God that she wasn't scared to tell me about Clyde.

"Nia, I need you to be honest with me. Did anything else besides touching happen with you and Clyde?"

Still sitting on the floor and looking up at me, she gave me a dead stare and angrily said, "No."

"Nia, tell me what exactly happened now. Because for months, I didn't question you. I believed you instantly off the merit of being my daughter. So many of my friends' moms didn't believe them. I said I would always believe my daughter. And that's why I got rid of Clyde. But what's happening with you? Your behavior is just escalating."

"I DON'T WANT TO TALK ABOUT IT!" she screamed loudly as she got up from the floor and sat on the far side of the bed.

I lost it and followed her to the other side of the bed and yoked her by the arm.

"Listen, little bitch, I don't care what you want to talk about. Now tell me what the fuck happened right now!"

"Get off of me! Get off of me!" she yelled and yanked away from my embrace. She jumped on her bed sheet and scooted up to the top of the bed. "Leave me alone!" she yelled.

"NIA, SHUT THE FUCK UP YELLING IN MY FUCKING HOUSE, YOU LITTLE BITCH! STOP THAT CRYING! SIT UP AND TELL ME WHAT THE FUCK HAPPENED RIGHT NOW BEFORE I GIVE YOUR ASS SOMETHING TO CRY ABOUT!"

Her body froze. She wiped her eyes and sat up.

"Mommy," she said in between whimpers, "the night before my graduation I was sleeping. I woke up and seen Clyde standing over me, rubbing my butt with one hand and his dick with the other. His face was so sweaty. When he saw me wake up, he tried to act like he was fixing his zipper. That's when I got out the bed and came in your room to get you."

I held my head in my hand the whole time while listening to her in disgust. Sadly, not disbelief. I believed every bit because Clyde was a nasty mothafucker. I knew that.

"Baby, I'm so happy you came to me. But please tell me, did anything happen before then that led up to this or after? Please tell me, baby girl, please. Maybe we can get you some help — a counselor or something, but you have to tell me everything," I pleaded.

"I told you, nothing else happened."

"Oh, thank God," I said as I sat down on the bed and embraced her from the back.

"Baby girl, without trust, we have nothing. Promise me you will never be scared to tell me anything ever again. I am your best friend. I am your biggest supporter, and I will be here until the end. Don't you forget that."

"Okay, Mommy, I won't," she said.

While part of me knew that Glo was genuinely concerned for Nia's wellbeing in this matter, a small hidden part in my gut told me that Glo was laughing at Nia's pain. In actuality, she was laughing at me for failing my daughter. Knowing this infuriated me. While Nia was trying so hard not to disappoint me, she was hurting me instead.

Having sex as a pre-teen wasn't the worst thing ever. Not having the right women in your corner to guide you and help you develop a healthy self-esteem was. I wanted to be Nia's first go to and number one confidant. I guess I should be thankful that Nia had someone else to confide in, even if it was my ghetto fabulous, hating ass sister.

CHAPTER 12

ORION'S BELT

Among ***Orion's*** *best-known features is the "****belt,****" consisting of three bright stars in a line, each of which can be seen without a telescope.*

I just had to get over it. My daughter was no longer a virgin. Saving her innocence was no longer an option. Within such a short period of time, she experienced so much. Her stepfather who raised her had groped her, and she contracted an STD her first time having sex. This pained me tremendously because I didn't know what to do. Not being able to relate to her caused me to have a hard time understanding or processing what she was going through and why she became so rebellious.

I could understand a teenage girl with a boyfriend rebelling against her parents, sneaking to his house, and kissing, touching or even having sex, but I couldn't imagine a twelve-year-old with no boyfriend, receiving no real male attention, being so boy crazy or promiscuous.

I did everything I could to shield Nia from the streets. I turned my life around after she was born. I got out of the streets and was climbing the corporate ladder of Accounting, doing Accounts Receivable chargebacks for fashion companies. I tried my best to drown out the horrors of the hood, for Nia.

Even with a crackhead mother, I was never molested or touched inappropriately by any of my mother's boyfriends or friends. Pam ran a tight ship. I didn't even know my mother was on drugs until I was fourteen. To this day, I never contracted an STD. The most I experienced was repetitive yeast infections from my dirty dick ex-boyfriend at the age of seventeen. Thinking of all of this just reminded me of how I was riding the failure train in parenting.

I tried so hard to be a better parent than Pam, to not let anything get in the way of me being a mother. Yet and still, I couldn't even protect my daughter.

* * *

On the weeks we didn't go out for lunch or dinner, Tony would come by and we usually went to a park and sat and talked. Today he picked me up around 6:30pm and instead of driving to the nearest park, we just sat in his SUV.

"Prison in de States is like eh tree star hotel stay compared to prison inna Jamaica. At least yuh get a mattress fuh sleep pon. Me uh sleep pon de ground wid a likkle piece ah cardboard mi haf fuh beg $10 Jamaican dollas from mi bredren fuh. Gal yuh af no idea."

"Damn, that's tough, but ain't shit sweet about jail here. It's hard here too. Jail ain't the place for nobody, regardless of where it is in the world," I spat back at Tony.

These foreigners come here and swear we don't know struggle because we're born here.

"Listen gal, everyting easier in this abloodclot country. Me ah go tuh prison because mi and mi pickney haf no food and likkle money, no running wata. Gyal, yuh never go hungry a day in yuh life. Trust me, baby gal."

He was beginning to annoy me, and I just wanted to tune him out. The truth was, I did know what it was like to go without. Maybe not hungry, but that's because I refused to be. I'm cut from the kind of cloth that makes it happen. Not having money never stopped me. Either I was going to work for it or take it.

We may have disagreed on this issue, but Tony intrigued me more now than when we first met. Even slouching in his car seat, his head nearly hit the ceiling of the car. He inhaled a pull from the neatly rolled spliff before passing it to me. I grabbed it, took a pull, and looked out of the darkly tinted windows.

As I looked up to the nighttime sky, I saw a half moon set in the center of an Orion's belt of the three brightest stars shining down on me while I sat smitten with the next woman's husband.

"Gal, yuh nuh kno whet it like fuh walk barefoot? Mi ah walk every bloodclot place barefoot until mi ah turn eighteen year old. Mi remember one time mi head dung to ah party wid a nice browin'. Mi ah really like tis gal and want fuh impress she so mi ah go put pon mi brotha dem sneakers. Him come embarrass me at di likkle party saying, "Take off mi shoes brotha, take off mi shoes now." Joi, will yuh believe it? Mi own brother dem mek mi take off him shoes while he had two & tree pairs and mi nuh haf none. Shoes nuh easy fuh come by inna Jamaica. Mi own brotha dem mek me walk home beside him barefooted."

The water began to swell up in my eyes as I widened them. He was right. I had no idea what it was like to walk barefooted. How could a man who grew up walking barefoot on hard concrete be so gentle? Even his voice was light and soft.

He had opened up to me about his wife, his citizenship, and now even his childhood. I had yet to reveal much to him. While contemplating on how much I would share, Pam's words ran through my mind. *Always keep a little mystery with a man. The least he knows, the more he'll want you.*

"Wow. Barefoot? You really been through a lot. You're so strong," I said as I interlocked my hand in his and squeezed it tight.

He squeezed my hand back and chuckled. "Yea, gal. Past tings. Mi just give thanks to Jah for mi blessings," he responded as he raised his seat up to be leveled with mine. As the seat inched up, we caught direct eye contact. His stare was intense, and his eyes were tired but had a persistent light that peered through my soul.

"Sweet Joi, yuh nuh tell mi much, but based on what yuh say and whet ah cyan see, issa ah good look. Yuh young, hot gal, yuh working, a good job at tat, only one pickney, nuh criminal. Yuh got it gwan on, gal."

I couldn't help but blush. Clyde never bigged me up. He was with me because I was smart but hated when I went back to school. He was with me because I was a sexy PYT, but he was too insecure to shower me with compliments or show me off.

"Thank you, Mr. Tony Skank," I said shyly.

"Doh tink mi ah let yuh off di hook so easily, woman. Yuh tawk about jail as if yuh did some real time. When di last time yuh get locked up?"

Now he's getting a bit too personal. I didn't want to tell him the truth about the case I caught three years ago and that I was still on probation. So, I lied.

"Years ago. Before my daughter was born."

CHAPTER 13

INDIFFERENT

If you're indifferent about something, you don't care much about it one way or another.

Everybody lies, whether they mean to or not. Whether it's a big deal or a small lot. Sometimes we lie to protect people, but most importantly, to protect ourselves. Sometimes we omit the truth to avoid the trauma surrounding it. Interestingly enough, we tell the most truths when we are young. It's not until we grow older that we find the need to hide. We hide behind our pain, our laughter, and our illnesses.

Nia was stronger than me because despite how young she was, she didn't hide or lie. She came clean about everything. I had to commend her for that. I also couldn't hold a grudge against Pam any longer.

The next day while at work in my small Midtown Manhattan cubicle, I dialed Pam's number on my cell phone. It rang several times before going to voicemail.

"It's Pam. I'm not here to take your call. Leave me a message and I'll get back to you. Ciao."

"Ma. Call me back."

Before I could put my cell phone away in my purse, it began to vibrate. I looked at the screen that read "Mom Dukes."

On the second ring, I answered, "Hey, Ma."

"Joi, it's your sister."

"What's up Glo, where's Pam at?"

"She's getting her blood taken. I'm at the doctor's office with her. I'll have her call you back."

"Cool," I answered before hanging up.

What was really the point of Glo calling me back just to tell me she'd have Pam call me back? I refused to believe that she just wanted to hear my voice. She called me back to make her presence known. Since we were kids, she would always try to one up me. She knew that I handled most of Pam's business. She wanted to gloat about taking Pam to the doctor to make me jealous when I couldn't care less. Of course, Glo went with Pam to the doctor — it was midday on a weekday. I was at work, and I didn't remember the last time Glo was employed.

A few hours later as I was packing up my belongings at work, my cell phone began to ring again.

"Hey, Ma, what's up?" I answered.

"Joi, come down to the projects. Gloria's here. I need to talk to you both."

I rolled my eyes and sucked my teeth as I stared intently out of the window into the sky turning to dusk. Fall was approaching. It was nearly dark before six pm.

"Don't come here with that attitude of yours either.It's important."

"Okay, Ma. I'm on my way. I'll have Nia meet me there.

"Don't worry; Nia's here already. You just get yourself here."

I hung up confused as to why Nia was at Gloria's house. I told her to come home after school every day. I rushed to the elevator of my building, took it to the lobby, and briskly walked to the nearest train station. I couldn't take anymore secrets.

* * *

When I walked into the apartment, it was awfully brighter than my last visit. Glo was sitting in the dining area adjacent to the small, cut off kitchen on a black bar stool.

"'Sup, Glo? Where's Nia? Where's Pam?"

"Pam's in the bathroom and Nia's across the building at Patience's house."

"Nia's on punishment. She's not allowed to hang out after school. She's supposed to come straight home," I said.

"Yeah, yeah. Looks like she didn't listen to her Mommy," she mocked.

As I walked further into the living room to take a seat on the couch, Pam appeared. She was wearing black leather pants and an oversized white shirt. She was the thickest I'd ever seen her in years since she got clean. It was nice to see her looking and feeling good.

"Sista Suki!" she exclaimed as she walked over to me and gave me a peck on the cheek.

"Hey, Ma. How you feeling? I called you earlier to just apologize about the last time I was over your house. I was trippin'."

"I'm feeling okay, Joi, and don't worry about it," she said in a low mutter. She began to twiddle her thumbs and look down at the floor.

"I wanted you both together so I could tell you something very important."

"Ma, I already know, so just go on and tell Joi," Glo said in an irritating tone.

I rolled my eyes and turned my back completely to Glo. *Why does she have to be such a bitch?*

"Listen, baby girl. I have Hepatitis C, and I've had it since the 80s. When I first got it, the doctors told me it wouldn't bother me until I got into my 50s. The doctor just told me I have to start dialysis next Monday. I'll have to do it three times a week, and I'ma need you girls to work together to help your mother."

My eyes were already watery after she revealed having Hep C. Tears began to fall once she said the word dialysis. It took such a huge toll on the body.

I turned my body to face both Glo and Pam respectfully.

"Of course, Ma, whatever you need," I responded. I scooched closer to Pam on the couch and grabbed her hand and held it tight. I leaned in and hugged her. Her body was so warm. She wrapped her arms around me tightly and kissed me on the forehead.

"Umm, Joyce-Ann speak for yourself. Don't make plans for me. Pam, I spent all of my 20s taking care of your son while you were in the drug program. I can't take care of you and my son now."

"He's not just her son. He's also our little brother, and you're not the only fucking one who raised him. And you damn sure ain't the only one with a kid. Stop making excuses, Gloria. Our mother is sick, and she needs us!" I spat back.

"Joi, fuck you. I was the one at the hospital with her earlier, so you don't tell me about excuses. Her son, our brother, whatever you wanna call him LIVED with me and visited you. There is a difference, and don't you ever forget it."

"Yeah, but I'm the reason he's in college right now and can make something of himself. No need to go tit for tat but if you want to- we sure can. Consider a favor for a favor since you like keeping records. While you ran the streets, Mommy took care of your son, so you helped out with hers when she needed you. Let it go."

"Don't tell me to let go of shit. At least I ain't get arrested and had to have my baby in jail, you unfit mothering bitch!"

Before I knew it, I jumped up in Glo's face and grabbed her by the neck. Her feet instantly began to dangle from the bar stool.

"Pam, you better get your daughter before I kill this bitch and end up back in jail."

Pam got up slowly but yelled frantically, "Joi- Ann let go of her! Let go of her! Now! Stop this fighting, right now!"

My hold was so tight around Glo's neck as she gasped for air in between the curse words flying out of her mouth. She looked me dead in the eye before she spat in it.

"You nasty bitch!" I yelled as I jumped back.

Pam stood in front of me with her hands stretched out, trying to protect me from Gloria.

"STOP THIS SHIT NOW! FIGHTING IS FOR ANIMALS! STOP IT NOW, GIRLS!" Pam pleaded.

"I'm giving you one minute to get the fuck out of my house now!" Glo barked.

ALTHOUGH A LITTLE FLUSTERED, I started patting down my clothes, undoing the wrinkles in the dress shirt and slacks. I dug in my pocket to feel my cell phone and car keys. I was prepared to leave.

"Gloria, sit yo' ass down. This is my apartment that I raised both of you in. I invited Joi here to talk to you both about ME, and I'ma do it right here and both of you heifers is gon' listen. Now hear me clearly; I am going to need you two to come together, rotate whatever the hell you want to do to make sure I get dialysis three times a week. Now, can you do that?"

"Of course, Mommy," I instantly responded. Pam looked at me with a heartfelt smile and said, "Thank you, baby girl. I love you."

"If I'm not busy, I'll see what I can do. Now, are we done with this little meeting? I've already missed the first quarter of the Lakers game fucking around with y'all." Glo whined.

* * *

SOMETIMES I TRULY HATED GLORIA. How could she be so selfish? Pam wasn't the best mom, but she wasn't the worst — especially to Glo. While I was running the streets, boosting and being grown as a teenager, Pam treated and spoiled Glo just for listening.

Why did she have to be such a bitch?

Unfortunately for me, I didn't even have anyone to share my grief with but Nia. I so badly wanted to talk to Tony, but I just didn't feel comfortable. He didn't know my mother was an ex-crackhead, and I just didn't want to reveal it. I didn't want him to see me as human with some of the same problems that many people faced. I wanted him to continue to see me as his prized possession, so certain topics were just off-limits. Being with Tony was to escape my problems, not dwell on them.

The next time Tony and I had lunch, I just couldn't hold it in. We met on a Thursday afternoon when the weather was chilly, and the air was pretty breezy. The trees were bare of any leaves while the clouds drooped in the sky, preparing for the day's pouring rain. Luckily, we beat the showers.

We met in Midtown at a local Thai restaurant that I asked him to try. Frankly, I was tired of Ital and vegetarian food, so I made sure there was fish on the menu at the Thai spot.

Tony was dressed in his work clothes. Rugged jeans and construction boots full of paint and sheetrock residue stained his outfit from head to toe. Surprisingly, his black Kangol hat looked freshly crisped as if it just came out the box. Although we stood in a bustling restaurant in the heart of Hell's Kitchen, surrounded by business tycoons, Tony stood amongst them all with a cool confidence as if he belonged. It turned me on so much.

As soon as we both sat down and could look at the menu, Tony grabbed my hand.

"Babes! Ah tiyad of eating tis dirty food outside hea. I go cook someting nice fuh yuh and Nia. Bring yuh mommy too. That would be nice."

I instantly began to worry. To be frank, I wasn't ready for him to meet Nia or be up close and personal with Pam just yet. I pretended to ignore him, hoping he would let it go. He didn't.

"Babes! Ah serious. Set up di ting. Ah go cook fuh yuh mommy and yuh baby." He chuckled and his big smile widened. I hung my head down and turned my face opposite of him.

"Joi babes, what's wrong?" he asked.

I sat still for a moment. My body tensed up, and I held my hands tightly together before looking directly in his eyes.

"Aside from the fact that I'm not comfortable with you being around Nia like that just yet, Pam is sick."

"Okay, babes, we can plan for when she feels better."

"That won't be for a while. She's doing dialysis three times a week, and she's really drained the other days.

"Dialysis? What's that, babes?"

"It's a procedure to clean your blood that flows in you," I answered very shortly.

"Oh wow. Neva hear of such ah ting. How dat happen? I hope she gets better," he said sincerely and covered my hand in his. I quickly snatched my hand from his embrace.

"She won't. It happens when you spend your early teens shooting dope and your twenties and thirties smoking crack."

I couldn't believe a forty plus-year-old man didn't know what dialysis was.

Tony looked at me intently and said, "We have crackheads in Jamaica, babes. Mi understand."

"Was your mother one? Did she steal your shit and sell it? Did she always demand money from your friends anytime they came to visit, or when she saw them in the streets?

Tony remained quiet and continued to stare at me.

"Okay, then. You don't understand."

Tony began to smirk. He took a deep breath before closing and opening his eyes.

"No, mi might not undastand fully, but mi know wah it's like fuh be poor. Poor people dem haf it just as bad as crackheads. In Jamaica, di poor people haf it worse than di crackheads. At least the fiends dem can afford their needs," he said before laughing hysterically. I didn't find anything funny at all. I just sat there, unfazed and unmoved.

Yeah, he didn't understand like most foreigners didn't.

As soon as I got back to the office, I noticed the blinking red light on my office phone. I picked up the phone and pressed the voicemail button.

"Joi, I called your cell phone five fucking times. It's about your mother. Call me back."

I grabbed my cell phone and flipped it open. The glaring message read "5 missed calls" with Glo's name under it.

I was so enthralled in my lunch date that I hadn't noticed my phone vibrate. To be honest, even if I had, I probably wouldn't have answered for Glo.

I dialed her back on my cell and it rang two times before she answered.

"Joi, what the fuck? I been calling you. This dialysis shit is taking a really bad toll on Pam. This is her third time going this week, and she's out of it. No energy and she may have to stop working."

"I was at a lunch meeting with my boss and some colleagues. Sorry for missing your calls. Dialysis is exhausting. It's a blood transfusion multiple times a week. If it's too much for her to work, then she may have to apply for Social Security. Now is not the time for Pam to be living alone. Moving in with you would be ideal. She won't have to walk up those stairs, and you can tend to her needs during the day. I'll come by after work and weekends to help and take her to appointments and such.

We just have to work together to make her comfortable."

"Here you go, Joi, volunteering my services and now my house. I haven't had a free house for me and my son since our brother went off to college. Why the fuck she can't come stay with you on Marion Street? You know Pam don't like staying here 'cause it remind her of her crack days. You the smarter one with a steady job. You can handle most of this shit."

"Gloria, stop the fucking bullshit. I don't have an elevator in my building, and there are four flights of stairs over here. She might as well stay at her place if she's gonna come here. Same difference."

"Exactly. I'm cool with that. She can stay at her place, and I'll visit her every other day."

"Gloria, you're such a selfish ass bitch. Pam is in no state to be staying alone. She needs someone to help her. If our brother wasn't away at school, it may have worked for her to stay home. But that's not the case. It's time for you to step up. Time for all of us to step up.

"I don't need you telling me nothing. Focus on what you will be doing. 'Cause if she stays with me, I have to tend to her all day."

"Okay and? You ain't doing shit else. Like you said, I'm the one with a job, so what the fuck is the problem, Gloria? This is our mother we are talking about. And once she gets Social Security, we can get her a home health aide to help with certain stuff! C'mon, Glo, we gotta stick together for Pam."

"YEAH OKAY, JOI."

That same indifference that Glo displayed on the phone showed up again and again the next week when Pam went to stay just a few days with her. We hadn't even moved her stuff in before I got a call at work from Pam, sobbing.

Unknowingly, I picked up the phone excited.

"Hey, Ma. I'm coming straight after work with your favorite — Red Lobster!"

I heard heavy sobbing on the other end.

"Ma. Is that you? Are you okay?

"Joi. I fell! I - I- I was going to the bathroom, and my legs gave out. I've been on the floor for two hours. Glo hasn't been here all day, and she's not answering the phone."

CHAPTER 14

HECTIC

Things that are hectic tend to happen quickly and all at once.

Think! Think! Think, Joi! What to do? Call Glo. Maybe she can get there fast. Nah. Fuck Glo. This is all her fault anyway. Okay cool. I'll call the ambulance and have her taken to the nearest hospital. I'ma leave work and head there now.

It took me an hour and forty-seven minutes to reach the hospital. I left work around 3:10pm and rushed to the A train, hoping the Express would get me there in forty-five minutes. Instead, I was met by congestion and crowdedness. The train was also stuck between the tunnel coming into Broadway Nassau for thirty minutes.

On the walk up Albany Avenue towards Interfaith Hospital, I called Glo. She didn't answer the first time or the twelfth time. However, on the seventh try, she began forwarding my calls to voicemail. Part of me really hoped she beat me to the hospital.

To my surprise, she didn't. By the time I made my way through the beige halls and the stale and desolate hospital musk to Pam's bed side, Gloria still hadn't appeared.

Upon entering the hospital room, I could see Pam sleeping with an IV in her left forearm. I turned around and walked out in search of a nurse or doctor. I walked briskly towards the nurse's station that stood about twenty or so feet down the hall.

"Where's the doctor for Pamela Holloway?" I asked the first nurse I saw sitting behind the desk. She was staring at her computer screen with her glasses lowly tilted.

"Dr. Kaster will be over to you in a minute," she responded without even looking at me.

"Are you sure that's even the right doctor? You didn't even look."

"Dr. Kaster will be with you shortly," she responded again as she quickly looked me in the face yet darted her eyes back to her computer screen.

Bitch.

I turned around and headed back to Pam's section. As I pulled back the curtain, she was attempting to turn over.

"Ma. Are you okay?"

"No, Joi, but I'm managing," she said as she laid back on her side and gave out a loud groan.

"DOCTOR! DOCTOR!" The same bitch nurse sitting at the nurses' station about twenty feet away looked in my direction.

"We need help!"

"Joi. Relax. They are doing their best. Don't worry. Look here baby, when Bobby calls, I need you to let him know everything the doctor tells you. Look in my bag for my phone."

"Ma. Puhlease. The last thing on my mind is Bobby!"

Seconds later, a short, stubby Jewish man with a beer belly waddled in and pulled the curtain back quickly. I looked up startled, and quickly shut the curtain behind him.

"Hi, I'm Joyce-Ann Holloway, Pamela's daughter. I understand that she fell. What's going on here? I was at work when it happened."

"Ms. Holloway, your mother suffered from a pretty severe hip fracture, and she's going to need immense physical therapy. Luckily, surgery is not needed, but she will be bedridden for a while until she can complete PT. I understand that she also does dialysis three times a week, correct?"

"Yes, she does."

"Between the fracture and dialysis, her best bet is to stay in a rehabilitation center at least for the duration of her hip to heal. They have some really nice ones that administer dialysis services as well."

I was speechless. It hadn't even been a full month since Pam had started dialysis, and now, she had to be admitted into a nursing home. This was all Gloria's fault. She had one fucking job! JUST ONE and she couldn't live up to that.

This would have never happened if Pam was living with me. Damn New York City apartments never have elevators unless it's in the projects. If only I had a house where she could have comfortably walked in, avoiding flights of stairs, this could have been avoided.

TWO MONTHS LATER...

Building a routine around my work schedule, Nia's school and after-school schedule, and now Pam's visiting hours at the nursing home was a great feat. Seeming as New York City parking is ridiculously expensive and unreliable, I never drove to work in Midtown. Instead, I parked my car near the last stop in Brooklyn. By 6pm, I was on the A Train headed to Jay Street to pick up my car and rush to the nursing home, which was settled in the quaint, residential area of Cobble Hill. I would visit four times a week and have Nia meet me there twice out of the week. The other days, she tended to her after school program.

Mondays, I was recharged from the weekend. Tuesdays, I was still chipper. By Wednesday, I was beat. Sometimes the traffic of rush hour delayed me, and I wouldn't get to Jay Street until a quarter to eight, yet visiting hours were over at 8:30pm, and the facility closed at nine. Those nights, I would still take the trip to either pick up Nia or just say hi.

On the days I missed the visiting block, I was always relieved, simply because I hated the smell of the nursing home. The sickly stench reeked of a combination of mildew and urine. The less time I had to spend there, the better. I specifically made sure to avoid bumping into Glo. I didn't want to see her at all.

TWO MONTHS LATER...

We hadn't spoken in about two weeks. Once she was made aware of Pam's arrangements, I kept my distance. I was done with the phoniness and the pretending. I didn't fuck with her. She left Pam for dead. I could never forgive her, but I'd tolerate her for the sake of Pam.

Knowing that Pam was okay, in her right mind, and progressing in physical therapy, relieved me. There was hope that as soon as she restored her hip, we could bring her home and hire a Home Health Aid to take her to dialysis, freeing up Gloria's schedule and my conscience. Although dialysis was physically draining on Pam's body, she still lit up the room with her vivacious smile every time she saw me.

"My joy, my joy, my joy who brings me joy," she'd say whenever I stepped into her nursing room.

I'd walk over to her bed and lean in for a peck. She was always so happy to see me. On the days when Nia wasn't there and I successfully avoided Glo, we talked and laughed. I brought her tasty food, and we ate and drank until she fell asleep.

Every visit, she asked the same questions: "How's my baby girl?" and "How's your tall guy friend?" I filled her in on every intricate detail regarding Nia but kept it short and sweet with Tony. As much as I knew Pam loved me and I was her favorite child, she couldn't hold water. She'd tell me Gloria's business and Gloria my business, and I just didn't want Glo knowing that Tony was married. I figured that not talking about him would decrease the likelihood of Glo finding out. That's if she didn't know already.

Things seemed to be working just fine between me and Glo. We only spoke about what Pam needed, and Glo was on top of the responsibilities she agreed to. She seemed more cheerful to witness Pam immobile than when she was walking and kicking at her house. The fact that she took delight in seeing her own mother in pain made me cringe. My heart burned with anger towards her. She disgusted me. Her nonchalance was a huge turn off, and I just wanted to avoid her altogether. Besides, I had my own problems to worry about and my own business to situate.

Shortly, after Pam fell, I was issued an order by my probation office to complete a drug program for marijuana use. My urine came back dirty a few months ago, and the program finally started. I was supposed to report there three times a week, but between work and visiting Pam, I'd only been able to make it twice a week. Pam really needed me, and I had proof that my mom was bedridden and sick. It shouldn't have been a problem.

Juggling the drug program also added to me being extremely overwhelmed. I spent most of my days traveling back and forth from one location to the next. It got a tad bit difficult to keep a tight leash on Nia. I just had to trust that she was at her after school program when she said she was. Frankly, I didn't have the time to double check and call. Those few hours went by so fast — especially when your phone was going in and out of service and you were bustling from train to train.

Today was one of those days I had to truck it to the drug program anyway. I hated going. It was such a waste of time. I wasn't an addict. The nine other people attending were addicts.

After work, I arrived at the Old Catholic Church on Meserole Avenue in Brooklyn a bit earlier than the seven pm meeting. The church was made of brick and marble and had a gloomy overcast. It was also in need of a few repairs as scaffolds surrounded the first half of the building. Approaching the entrance, I noticed that the heavy wind caused the chippings on the red door to shed. I pulled the handle and stepped inside. Instantly, my energy began to change. The air of melancholy combined with the dim lights festered a somber and despair feeling in my soul.

I can't wait for this shit to be over.

I proceeded down the dim hallway into the meeting room — an open area with just chairs. The walls were stark white, and the lights happened to be super bright.

Behind the desk stood my probation officer, Ms. Armstrong Wallace. Literally the darkskin version of Ms. Piggy, Ms. Armstrong Wallace was cool. I normally didn't like women in law enforcement. I preferred male COs too, but I couldn't lie; I had no reason to dislike Ms. Wallace.

She held three manila folders in her hand as she turned to me and said, "Hi Ms. Holloway. We'll be starting shortly. Take a seat as we wait for the others to linger in."

"Hi Ms. Armstrong, no problem. I wanted to make sure I wasn't late; that's why I'm here a bit early.

"Not a problem. Just take a seat."

I turned around and walked over to the chairs. They were white too and uncomfortable. I would have rather stood, but if Ms. Armstrong would have told me to take a seat again, I would've been visibly annoyed, so I just sat my ass down on the hard, sturdy chair. As soon as I sat down, in came Miranda, the white, twenty-seven-year-old meth head from Alphabet City. Dressed in light blue jeans and a dark patchwork denim jacket, her hair was slicked back in a messy bun. She nodded her head and raised her hand toward me. I guess that was her way of saying hello. I just nodded back.

She sat down across from me, twiddling her thumbs and biting her nails. It was a disturbing sight to watch. I just closed my eyes and tried to rest them despite the strong, beaming light in the room.

I was startled by the Latina dope grandmas, Luz, Carmen, and Ana who scurried in slowly yet finicky. They all naturally leaned sideways and walked with a limp. Aside from that, they were clean, their hair was done, and they all wore a different perfume scent. Luz wore White Diamonds by Elizabeth Taylor. It was easy to sniff out that scent anywhere. Carmen was dressed kind of sexy, wearing a low-cut shirt and leather high-waisted pants. You could tell she was a hot mami back in her days.

Ana addressed me for them all. "Hi, Bonita. Happy Day to you."

"Hi, ladies. Same to you," I responded.

Seconds later, the oreo crackhead crew came strolling in. John, Pete, Tom, and Sam walked in, cracking jokes on each other and laughing loudly.

"Hello hello, my dear sweet ladies. How is y'all doing tah-day?

"Okay, Sam," we all responded in unison as he chuckled.

Ms. Armstrong Wallace walked over to the center of our Kumbaya circle.

"Now that everyone is here, I would like to start this week's session off kind of differently. We normally talk about the struggles many of you have while trying to avoid using. Other than drugs, what else is going on with you? I just want you to know that your participation is expected. So, I will be calling on each of you to share with the group. Let's start with someone who is often quiet. Joi, how's your week going?"

I was not surprised that she called my name. I looked up and darted my eyes around the circle with a tight grin on my face, contemplating on whether or not I should give in and talk about what was really stressing me out or pretend that everything was fine.

Fuck it! What do I got to lose? Expressing myself back in group therapy when I was in prison, pregnant with Nia, always did relieve me.

"My week has been hectic. About a month before I started the program, my moms got admitted into the nursing home. She's a recovering addict and now has Hep C, which she has to do dialysis for. It takes a huge toll on her, and it's only me and my sister — well, really me 'cause my sister is a bitch and doesn't really care about what happens to my mother either way. It's actually her fault moms is in the nursing home. It's just been very stressful and overwhelming juggling my schedule, looking after my daughter, and now taking care of my mother. I'm down at the nursing home four times a week. I never thought I'd be taking care of my mother so soon."

"What makes you say it was your sister's fault that your mother is in the nursing home?" Ms. Armstrong asked inquisitively.

I didn't expect this to turn into a dialogue. I honestly expected to hear, "I'm sorry you're going through this." Her audacity to pry instantly put me on guard.

"Well, my mom was staying at my sister's house because as a family, we all decided it would be conducive because there's an elevator in my sister's apartment building and not one in my mother's building. Walking up four flights of stairs was just too much. My mother fell and broke her hip. By the time she got to call me, she had been on the floor for two hours. Even before she fell, she was calling my sister, and she never answered. I had to call the ambulance from work to go pick her up. My sister was supposed to be there. Mommy needed her. This could have all been avoided if she was there."

"Or if you were there too," a low voice muttered.

Before I turned my head to see who it was, Ms. Armstrong Wallace said, "Speak up, Miranda, so we can hear you."

Miranda shook her head and fidgeted her hands signaling no.

"Uhh, all I'm saying is, it's no more her fault than it is yours. You weren't there either."

After Miranda spoke, she shot me a stone-cold stare, then instantly looked down at the floor.

"But I was at work," I spat back angrily.

"Doesn't matter. You still weren't there. Maybe if you didn't work, you could have stayed home with your mom to give your sister a break. The point is, you weren't there either. Accountability. That's something Ms. Wallace talks about a lot here. We have to take accountability for our part in it.

"She's right, Joi. Instead of blaming your sister, understand that this is a lot on both of you and that really, it's nobody's fault, just an unfortunate circumstance. Your sister has to take accountability for not being there when she should have, and you have to take accountability for not being able to be there. All truth. All logic. No emotions," Ms. Armstrong said, jumping to Miranda's defense.

This is exactly why I didn't want to share anything in this fucking group. You teach a meth head a new vocabulary word and they think it applies to everything. This with Glo is not about accountability. It's about Gloria's carelessness and nonchalance.

"Yeah, yeah whatever. Like I said, if my sister was at home with my mother as planned, this could have been avoided. I don't need no fucking strangers telling me nothing. Listen and nod your heads like I do. Please and thank you."

"Listen, Listen, Bonita, trust me I understand. Pero, I blamed my bitch ass brother for my mother dying for years and this was back in the early eighties. I just had to accept that during the time my mom was sick, I was drugging, clubbing, and having the best time of my life. I didn't even think about my mother. Then, I wanted to blame my brother, who was there more than me. I learned that that's not the way life works, Bonita. You have to take responsibility for your part."

"Okay, great. Can we talk about someone else now?" I said, irritated through a big, sarcastic smile.

"Yes, of course, we can move on to the next person. If you can all keep your comments to yourself, that would be great. We don't want anyone to feel attacked. This is a judgment free zone."

Ms. Armstrong Wallace snapped her finger in my direction. I quickly glanced in her direction as she silently mouthed the words "I got you" to me. I smiled and just remained quiet, literally dying for the session to end.

I clocked out mentally for a bit as everyone talked about their week struggled to not get high or hang with people who got high. I was so lost in my own thoughts that I didn't hear Ms. Armstrong Wallace dismiss the group. I snapped back into the moment once I saw the oreo crackhead crew get up from their seats.

I began to get up and put my coat on.

"Thanks for sharing today, Joi. I'll be sure to tell the judge about your mom. He should be lenient about you only attending two times some weeks."

"Thank you, Ms. Armstrong. I really appreciate it."

Although I dreaded going to the drug program, I left feeling better. For once, I didn't feel threatened by law enforcement. I can honestly say that today's session helped me.

I guess therapy isn't that bad, even if it's amongst heavy drug addicts.

As soon as I walked out of the church, my phone rang, and the caller ID read "Home."

"Mommy, where you at?"

"On my way home, baby girl. How was school today?"

"School was okay. I can't stand my computer teacher, but I'll tell you later when you get home."

"Okay, chickenhead. You better be listening to your teacher. I'll see you soon," I said before I hung up.

Once in front of my apartment building door, my body began to relax. That was a signal that I was happy to be home after a long day. Once inside my building, I used my key to open my mailbox and the first envelope I saw said *Department of Probation.*

Oh boy.

I snatched the envelope and added it to the pile in my arm. As soon as I got to the fourth floor, I began to fumble for the key in my pocket. Anxious to get inside because I had to pee, I rushed to the bathroom as soon as I opened the door. Luckily, my bathroom was literally across from the front door. You couldn't miss it.

Relief settled in when I sat on the toilet. I tore the envelope open to find a letter addressed to me in bold caps "JOYCE-ANN HOLLOWAY VS. THE STATE OF NEW YORK. The next line read, "YOU'VE BEEN SUMMONED TO COURT FOR REFUSAL TO REPORT TO MANDATED PROBATIONARY DRUG PROGRAM."

Ahh what the fuck? I just left that fucking place.

CHAPTER 15

STINKIN' THINKING

The American psychologist Albert Ellis is credited with coining the phrase 'stinkin' thinking' to describe the human tendency to persistently engage with thoughts that do not serve them.

Probation and parole are by far the worst record keepers in law enforcement. When you're on probation or parole, the Department of Corrections own you. Luckily, I was charged with a misdemeanor, and I could still travel – unlike those on felony probation. However, I still had to adhere to invasive and intrusive drug testing. Every time I had to get my urine checked, the lab workers made me use the bathroom with the door open. You would have thought I robbed a bank. Truth was, I never did more than three years in jail consecutively.

Just like God, prison had no favorites. Once inside, it didn't matter if you were a shoplifter or a murderer, you were looked at and treated the same, like a menace to society and scum of the earth. There was no graduating from prison either, especially if you were still on probation. It wasn't until you were cleared from governmental monitoring that you could gain your freedom and liberty back.

After Nia was born, I had little to no police contact until I got caught up three years ago at my last job. I couldn't help myself. My co-worker went downstairs to her car one day and left her pocketbook on her desk. The stinkin' thinking started to creep in, and all I could think about as soon as she got up was her wallet.

Italian bitch probably got three to four valid credit cards in her bag right now.

Before I could stop myself, I jumped up and quickly rummaged through her bag. I removed two of her credit cards and neatly put her wallet back. Immediately after work, I rushed to Macy's in Herald Square and maxed out her cards. I walked out of that store with over three grand worth of merchandise — clothes for me and Nia, clothes for Pam and even Clyde.

In my reckless days, I would have gone joyriding with her cards, hitting various stores and different boroughs, even heading to Paramus in Jersey. But I had to be smart. It was supposed to be a one-time flex.

Hit a department store like Macy's. Ball out one good time. Done.

Some people would have been scared of getting stopped in a huge store like Macy's, but not I. I was a professional thief. I got caught many times in Macy's before I knew all the loopholes and getaways. So, I wasn't afraid. I was just cautious, and I got away with it — for a while. I didn't wear any of my flashy stuff I stole to work. I kept it cool. They didn't bust me until eight months later. My co-worker did an investigation, and they had me on tape using her card. I got fired and booked for eighteen months. They reduced it to six months, which I served two years ago. Since being released, I'd been on probation. This drug program was really supposed to be the last condition I'd have to fulfill for my probation to be dismissed. I'd done everything else.

My urine came back dirty for THC, and they were treating me not only like a criminal but an addict as well. I'd never been arrested for a drug related charge. Mandating me to go to a drug program with people who did heavy narcotics was just to make an example out of me.

The judge who issued this drug program was a dick and super hard on petty crime. I never killed anyone. I never sold drugs. I wasn't a child molester or a terrorist. I was just a black woman who'd been tryna survive her whole life once her mom and dad's drug addiction spiraled outta control. I had to eat!

The truth was, I didn't have to steal that lady's credit cards. Yes, it was a rough month financially and I was catching up on older bills and paying current ones. However, that didn't excuse my behavior. I had a steady job that was paying me decent money just enough to pay my bills but not much outside of that. I was used to dressing nice, eating out, and getting my hair done. Once I completely stopped boosting, the extra money to dress lavishly wasn't there.

THE DAY I stole my co-worker's credit cards, I had twenty-four dollars in my checking account. My bills were paid. I had food in the house, and I just paid for a monthly MetroCard to get back and forth from work. But I really wanted to order Thai food for lunch that cost eighteen dollars, and I'd be stuck with six dollars left for the next two weeks.

That's when the stinkin' thinking started to seep in. It came like a lightening wave. It shocked me, and I was affected. I did what came to me naturally. I did what any good thief would have done. First, assess the environment. Who was there and what belongings did they have? How loose were they with their belongings? Did they leave their bags out in plain sight or hide them?

Within my first week of starting the job, I scoped everyone out and learned their habits. For an entire year, I hadn't stolen from anyone on the job. I did think about it. Thoughts did run through my mind, but I resisted them because I was determined to keep a job for longer than three months and really become a career woman.

On that date I failed, and I gave in. I had a ball until I had to face the judge. Now having to deal with it two years later was a real drag. I was determined to successfully fulfill my probation requirements and be done with it. I'd just explain to the judge how severe my mom's condition was and why I'd been absent. Hopefully, he would see that I attended three times this week and give me some grace.

* * *

COURT WAS SET for seven days after I received the summons at eleven in the morning. Although I called out of work, I still dressed in work attire — slacks and a blazer while rocking my short haircut neatly in a flat wrap. I wanted to make a good impression. To play the part, you had to look the part.

The line to enter One Centre Street, the main courthouse for New York City, was protruding out of the building. I hated standing in that line, especially on cold days like today. Seven out of ten times you'd see a familiar face. My objective was to always avoid familiar faces. I didn't want to make conversation with anyone. I didn't need nobody prying in my business or wanting to know about my case. I pulled my sunglasses out of my bag, put them on my face, and held my head down.

Before I knew it, the line was moving, and I made it inside to the metal detectors. As a former inmate, courthouses never excited me.

The lighting was dim and the energy was concealed rage. The quicker in, the quicker I got out was always my motto. Regardless to how many people's cases I had to hear before mine, I just hoped to get seen before lunchtime.

I headed inside Courtroom Four, and to my surprise, there were only ten people inside, including the bailiff, the lawyers, and clients.

My public defender was a 5'3 overweight, Italian lesbian. She wore a messy short haircut, dark khaki pants, and a V-neck Polo shirt. I took a seat near her on the first bench.

With my file in her hand, she turned to me and said, "Joi. You'll be out of here in no time. You know this judge is a dick, but you were just at the drug program, so you'll be fine. You're second up after this prick," she said while sucking her teeth and nodding her head towards the couple in front of us — a young white lawyer dressed in a fitted suit and his older white client who had a caveman beard, and long dark hair.

"It literally came in the mail right after I got in from the drug program the other night. I was confused."

"Don't worry, Joi."

I wasn't worried. I sat patiently and was kind of happy I would have the rest of the day off of work as soon as I got out of there.

After counting the fifty stars on the American flag near the podium, eyeing how tight the bailiff's pants were, and hearing the young lawyer say "dude" about fifteen times, I was ready to go.

Finally, the judge walked in and the bailiff approached the judge's bench.

"All rise," the bailiff said.

We all got up and immediately sat back down.

"Joi-Ann Holloway vs. The State of New York," I heard loudly.

I was puzzled, so I turned to my lawyer.

"I thought we were second."

"Me too. Let's go. The quicker you're called, the quicker you can go home."

True.

I gathered my bag and followed my lawyer through the brown swinging doors towards the defendant's table.

My lawyer stood with her head leaned over the table as she sorted through her folders. The State public defender was actually the young white guy in a spiffy suit.

Despite how much power the judge had, he looked helpless trying to lengthen his neck to appear taller as he spoke.

"The People of New York State, speak your case."

"Your honor, the defendant is mandated to attend a drug program three times a week and out of twenty-four sessions, she's only attended fourteen times. As iterated in the file, she tested positive for THC twice. The first time, we gave her some leniency as she is an addict in recovery, but testing positive and not attending her mandated sessions is a concern for us.

"Indeed, it is," the judge said as he adjusted his glasses while writing notes on a pad.

"Defendant. Take the floor."

"Thank you, your honor. Although my client has missed some sessions in the past, she was present for all three sessions just last week. My client is the beneficiary and proxy to her mom, who is bedridden in a nursing home with a fractured hip all while going to dialysis three times a week. I can assure you that my client was not ditching her drug program responsibilities but simply getting acclimated to juggling her drug program schedule and her mother's visiting hours. Nonetheless, my client is making progress and will continue to attend all mandated sessions."

"Thank you, counselor. Take a seat please."

The judge closed his arms firmly and made a tight grin.

"Ms. Holloway, will you approach?

I got up quickly.

"Good day, Your Honor."

"Ms. Holloway, I find it interesting that while given grace for dirty urine TWICE while on probation, that you would miss one third of your mandated drug program sessions. Your complete lack of respect for authority is disheartening. I am convinced you take my fairness for weakness and that attitude must be corrected. I am ordering you to 180 days on Rikers Island. Once you are released, you will be done with probation and a fully free woman. This court is adjourned!"

I stood frozen. In shock. It wasn't until my lawyer approached me that I began to come back alive.

"How can they do this? I thought you said don't worry!" I screamed.

"I am sorry, Joi. I never saw this coming."

"Ms. Holloway, please stand." The bailiff approached the table.

Rage grew in my heart by the second. One slow tear fell down the right side of my face as I continued to sit obstinately in defiance.

"WHAT ABOUT MY DAUGHTER? WHAT ABOUT MY FUCKING MOTHER? YOU WHITE RACIST BASTARDS!"

The bailiff drew closer and grabbed me by my underarm.

"Let's go, Ms. Holloway."

CHAPTER 16

AGAINST THE GRAIN

very difficult for you to accept it or do it because it conflicts with your previous ideas, beliefs, or principles.

The worst part about getting arrested was the transport from the holding cell to the actual jail house. For some reason, you were never transported at night. They wanted you to see your freedom being taken away. Whether it was cold out or hot, the sun always reminded you of the reality that yet again, you were going to jail and that was rarely easily digestible.

Taking in the visual of barbed-wire fences and tall gates disturbed my spirit as I sat on the bus disappointed. My heart sunk. Why now? Pam was sick and needed me. Nia needed me.

After I was remanded, I had to think fast. I couldn't use my only phone call on Glo and risk her not answering, so I called Tony.

He answered on the second ring.

"Baby it's me, Joi. I got sentenced to 180 days at court today. I need you to come down here and get my keys and my car. Go to my house, wait for Nia to get there, then take her to Glo's house. Please, baby, I really need you. You're all I have right now."

"Baby love, oh gosh, tell mi wea fuh go. Mi uh cum dung rite now suh."

I gave him the address, and he rushed down to see me and retrieve my keys and my car. I wasn't shocked at his eagerness to help or his sense of urgency. I was, however, embarrassed.

The embarrassment I felt had nothing to do with being locked up but everything to do with the fact that I hadn't been forthcoming with my probation affairs, yet I needed him. I was relieved that he didn't interrogate me over the phone and just came to my aid.

Knowing I could rely on him made me fall deeper in love. It was already a thrill dealing with a married man, especially an unhappily married man. I felt as powerful as an antidote, curing his misery while simultaneously filling my selfish void to be needed, wanted, and desired. In the words of Pam, that was my fun in it.

But when I called him from the holding cell, it became evident that this adulterous affair was rooted in more than just sexual chemistry. It was rooted in love. Actionable love because when I needed him, he showed up, and that's what love is.

* * *

AIN'T NOTHING new under the sun and don't a damn thing change in jail. Same shit, different mess hall. Same COs, different hairstyle. The motto was in and out. Stay low and go. One hundred and eighty days, easy peezy lemon squeezy. I just wanted to go home to my baby, my momma, and my new man.

My first two days inside were full of panic. I was franticly awakened by a male CO at the crack of dawn. Luckily, I didn't have a cellmate. In fact, the jail was pretty quiet — the quietest I'd seen it. The line for the showers were a third of its usual length. Despite how many fewer inmates were there, the bathroom still reeked of piss, mildew, and an overcast of bleach.

Guck and grime were plastered deep in the crevices of every tile in the shower. The shower head was full of rust; the water pressure was immensely low while the temperature was scorching hot. Instead of standing under the fountain of water, I wet my rag, scrubbed my body, rinsed out my rag, and drained the water from the rag onto my body to wash away the remaining suds. I repeated this process over and over until I was soap-free. Had I stood under the shower head; I would have had a second-degree burn.

Tony left me just enough money to buy some hygiene products from the commissary and make a few calls. Nia was staying with Glo, and I needed to speak to her. Badly. I waited to call during the nighttime, assuming she'd be at school during the day.

I held my head down as I stood in line, waiting for the short Asian woman to wrap up her conversation. I made it a point to avoid eye contact unless spoken to. After waiting for what seemed like forever, the inmate in front of me finally slammed the phone onto the hook and stepped away.

I punched Glo's number in and after a brief pause, the phone began to ring.

"Hey, sister, wassup?" Glo said on the other end.

"Glo. I got jammed up at court on some probation shit. Thanks for looking after Nia."

"Save the thanks for ya little dread boyfriend. He was the one you called and trusted with your daughter. You don't even know this nigga."

"I couldn't risk my one phone call and you not answer," I spat back.

"Bullshit. Joi. Bullshit. You know damn well I would have answered a collect call. Your last pervert boyfriend was feeling her up. Then, you give some non-descript nigga your keys to wait at home for your daughter. What the fuck is wrong with you?"

"Listen, Gloria, I don't need your fucking judgment. I just need to speak to my daughter. Please, Glo. Where is she?"

"She's across the building at Patience's house."

"Glo, it's nine o'clock on a Wednesday night! What the fuck? And on top of that, you know I cut that shit out with Nia being in the projects and hanging with Patience months ago. I don't want my daughter out late on no school night."

"Pipe the fuck down. She's just across the building. She'll be back soon."

"What time is soon? I need to talk to my daughter."

"Her curfew is eleven o'clock."

"Eleven o'clock? She's fucking twelve years old. Listen, bitch. I need my daughter in the house no later than seven. One, because I need to talk to her, and two, because she's fucking twelve years old. Are you shitting me?"

"Joi, I gotta go. Call back tomorrow after eleven o'clock. She'll be settled in bed by then. Goodnight, bitch." She laughed and quickly hung up.

I was livid. Gloria had no regard for Nia's safety or my authority.

Instead of going to the community school across the street from Brevoort with all of the project kids, I sent Nia to school deeper in Bed Stuy — to me and Gloria's old elementary school where my Daddy was the President of the PTA when we were enrolled.

The teachers were more rooted, the academics were stronger, and Nia gained a sense of independence by taking the train a few stops to school, which definitely came in handy those days I was running late to work and couldn't drop her off. Gloria's son went to the community school while Nia attended our old school and even had the same fifth grade teacher as Gloria's.

I swear, Glo always had to go against the grain. That's exactly what she was doing by setting an eleven o'clock curfew for Nia. She knew what she was doing, and she was intending to mock me and undermine my parenting skills. I guess she figured since Nia wasn't a virgin that she might as well be allowed to stay out late.

To be frank, I didn't know, and I didn't care what she was thinking. It wasn't happening. I had to think quick. I had to put a stop to this now. Nia being under Glo's supervision was not ideal.

Damn, I wish Pam was home. Nia would have stayed with her. It had been days since I last saw or spoke to Pam. I didn't know how she was doing. I didn't even get a chance to ask Glo. Things went left so fast. At first, it crossed my mind that Pam probably had no idea I was locked up but then I remembered who my sister was. Gloria always delighted in reporting bad news about me. Not that Pam shouldn't know. But I wanted to be the one to tell her. Gloria didn't even get the details from me to pass on the right information to Pam.

I sighed just thinking about everything. Not that there's ever a good time to be in jail, but now certainly wasn't. I had too much shit on my plate. Too much to think about and too many tough decisions to make.

I was legally responsible for two people, and I was behind bars with no voice, no power, or authority to make decisions for myself, let alone someone else. As angry as I was at Glo, I was determined to let it go and give it to God before I headed back to my cell. I refused to go to sleep full of strife. I needed to brush off the drama and show a complete change of heart.

I was Daniel in the Lion's Den with my hand in the beast's mouth. The only way to avoid getting bit was to pull my hand out slowly and gracefully. I was determined to keep the peace with this bitchy sister of mine for one reason only — to speak to my daughter. Nothing was more important than that, and if I had to kiss Gloria's ass, I was prepared to.

* * *

THE NEXT DAY, I beat the guard and woke up while it was still pitch black outside. In jail, there was no concept of time. Jail was the only place where time was limitless and stoppable. If you were not allowed rec time to watch the news, then you'd have no idea of the date or month. Hints from the weather and scheduled block times for lunch may have given you some idea, but other than that, you were never certain. The saddest reality to face was that it really didn't matter. Keeping track of the time didn't make it go by any faster.

The only times I looked forward to were to shower time, going to commissary and making phone calls. Regardless of how many bids I did, visitation never excited me. I didn't want visitors. I wanted to go home. Every! Time! Visitation was too painful to witness and endure. I never wanted anyone to get comfortable or used to going through invasive body checks just to see me. I never wanted to get comfortable with looking forward to weekly visits. I wanted to do my time, go, and never return.

Showering, grocery shopping and talking on the phone gave me a sense of normalcy. Doing these things allowed me to channel my home environment. Seeing metal detectors, brick walls, and hearing the brass door open every thirty minutes as new visitors greeted their incarcerated loved ones angered, irritated, and gave me anxiety.

I didn't even want to see Nia. Maybe once or twice, but I would have been happy if she didn't show up. She didn't need to be consumed with my drama and what I had going on. She'd spent enough time here already. I just wanted to talk to her.

I made a vow when I became a mother that I would be together enough to not burden my daughter with my issues. I made a vow that I would shield her from the streets and protect her. I made a vow that unlike Pam, I would not put my daughter in a position where she had to fend for herself.

Pam was getting high and thought that providing a place to live and halfway decent advice was good enough. Considering how destructive the crack epidemic was for many poor families, in hindsight, it was enough. And it was the best she could do, but it wasn't the best I could do, and I refused to settle for less — especially when Nia and I were nothing alike and neither were our childhoods.

Pam was on crack, but what was my excuse for having my daughter in prison? What was my excuse for stealing my co-worker's credit cards? What was my excuse for being away from my daughter? Was it greed? Was it poverty? Was it my upbringing? Was it my self-esteem?

It was a combination of all — a lack of prioritizing responsibilities and the stinkin' thinking that seeped into my mind at the tender age of fourteen when I started boosting. Stinkin' thinking presented itself in many ways, in relation to many things, but mine was rooted in criminality, cutting corners, and getting over. I could confidently say that it was ruining my life in small, subtle ways.

It was time for it to stop. Luckily, it was almost over. After carrying out my sentence, I'd be done with probation and law enforcement in totality. Knowing that put me at ease. But I was on edge, having still not spoken to Nia. I needed to speak to my baby girl.

I decided to use my first phone call of the day to call Glo. I wanted to get on good terms with her first so by the time Nia got in from school, I could use all of the time on my evening call to talk with my baby girl. Glo didn't work, and visiting hours at the nursing home didn't begin until the afternoon, so I wasn't sure why she wasn't answering.

I tried not to panic and just returned to my cell and pulled out my Bible. I'd read the Bible twelve times from front to back. It was the only piece of literature worthwhile while on lockdown, in my opinion. When I returned for my evening call, Glo didn't answer again.

What the fuck, Glo?

I didn't want to involve Tony any further, but I literally had no one, and I hadn't spoken to my daughter since I got arrested.

Hesitantly, I picked up the headset and dialed Tony's number. He answered on the first ring.

"Babes, wah gwan? Yuh good?"

"No. I haven't spoken to Nia yet."

"How cum yuh nuh call pon yuh sista phone, babes?"

"Listen, my sister is on some bullshit. She got my daughter outside at all times of the fuckin' night, so when I called last night at nine o'clock, Nia wasn't in the house. I checked her about it, and she hung up on me. I've been calling her all day today and no answer. I just called her before I called you."

Tony cleared his throat and remained quiet until a low raspy, "Hmm" muttered out of his mouth.

Grief filled my heart; pain grew in my stomach as tears began to form in my eyes. I didn't notice I was sobbing until I heard Tony say, "Hush, gal. No cry."

"Babes. Wah yuh want mi fuh do? Just say di word."

I wiped the tears from my face with the back of my hand and leaned into the headset.

"Tomorrow, I need you to pick Nia up at her school. I need you to be there around two-thirty so you won't miss her before she heads for the train. Visiting hours are over at nine pm. Please bring her to me. I need to talk to my daughter."

CHAPTER 17

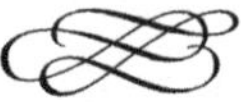

TWILIGHT

occurs just after sunset but before dawn; the time when something is declining or approaching its end, especially in a gentle or peaceful way.

I made a choice. I took a chance and all I wanted in return was a positive consequence. I knew it was risky inserting Tony again, but he was all I had, once again. Glo wasn't answering the phone. I took Nia's cell phone away months ago, and Pam's phone was disconnected while she was in the nursing home. Tony was my only lifeline.

It hurt to admit that Glo was right. I didn't know Tony that well and we weren't exclusive, but he showed up when I needed him most. When I called, he answered, and he was ready to help. He showed me things and gave me a new perspective on life in a matter of a few months that Clyde never even scratched the surface to convey or display in eleven years.

Tony's entire conversation differed from Clyde. He came from humble beginnings and believed in making an honest living. He got up every day before dawn to work a physically demanding job just to send two-thirds of his check to his kids in Jamaica. That's a real man. Clyde never maintained a job longer than two weeks, let alone years.

The only thing Clyde cared about was hustling. He wasn't into the news. He wasn't into his health. He didn't care about what he put in his body. Tony introduced me to eating healthier. He took me out of the country for the first time. Even in our conversations about jail, he never glorified it or gave me the inclination that I should sensationalize crime and jail. Tony allowed me to be a lady, and it felt so damn good.

Even behind bars, he still humanized and feminized me. He wanted to protect me from ever returning to prison again. When I initially got arrested three years ago for this case, Clyde not only smuggled in weed for me to smoke every visit; he also smuggled in weed for me to sell, which ultimately was a huge risk to my freedom. I didn't care about me and neither did Clyde. Had we been together now, Clyde would have definitely suggested that I make some side money inside. Fortunately, I didn't have to worry about Tony suggesting anything of that sort. I could do my bid in peace without negative pressure or stinkin' thinking.

Unable to sleep, I stayed up contemplating if I was making the right choice by asking Tony to pick Nia up from school. I figured they got acquainted the last time Tony took her to Glo's house, but I truly had no idea how Nia would react. It had only been three days, but I felt like I hadn't spoken to my baby in forever. She was changing and growing every day. I couldn't imagine what was going on in her adolescent head. Between being molested, losing her virginity, catching an STD and now dealing with a mom in jail, I knew she was going through a lot, and I just wanted to talk to her. I just wanted to get into my baby's head to see what she was thinking and try to correct it.

Although it hadn't been long, I knew I had some reprogramming to do for Nia. I had no idea what Gloria was saying, doing, or teaching my baby. But I knew my sister, and she was not a good influence on Nia. For the most part, I knew Glo was going to feed my baby and send her to school well dressed. I knew Glo cared about the general welfare of Nia, but I also knew that we differed in our parenting approaches. It was clear to me that Glo was more concerned with being the cool, fun Auntie than shielding and protecting the innocence of her niece.

Glo's snarky comments about Nia losing her virginity gave me the indication that she didn't see her niece as an inexperienced, innocent preteen. It seemed as though she felt that Nia should have been treated as an eighteen-year-old, especially with an eleven o'clock curfew. And that was where she was wrong.

* * *

THE BANG at the cell door startled me, and I dropped my book. I quickly looked up as I watched the door slowly slide open. On the other side stood two people, a tall white male CO and an average height overweight woman. She held her head down, preventing me from seeing her face. Since there was still sunlight outside, the lights were off in the cell, creating a dim overcast. They were too far away to fully see the depth in their faces.

"Inmate. Meet Inmate. Get cozy," the CO said. He released his grip from her arm and quickly turned around. He rushed out of the cell and shut the door.

As the woman walked towards the bed opposite of me, her stench became more pronounced and smacked me in the face so hard I flinched. I couldn't make out her exact odor. She'd have to move around a bit more. She continued to hold her head down and didn't say a word. I remained quiet as well. When someone entered the room, they should address you. Not the other way around. Besides that, normally in jail when people don't speak first, they don't want to be spoken to. I understood and respected that.

I scooted to the edge of my bed to reach for my book. My cellmate lightly kicked it in my direction. That slight motion revealed her repulsive odor — a mix of musk, funk, and fish. Without trying to offend, my natural reflex made me cover my nose. It happened so fast. I didn't expect to not have a cellmate for too long. I'd had my share of them, but this was by far the worst first impression a cellmate could make.

"Doh worry, gal. I soon shower. Mi fresh scent is much sweeter," she said in a Caribbean accent. I didn't recognize it. It was too soft to be a Jamaican accent and too sweet for a Bajan accent, so I was confused.

"I hope so," I nonchalantly replied.

She finally looked up and that's when I caught a glimpse. Her face was round, and her cheeks were plump. You could tell that she had lost a few pounds, considering the hallow space and loose skin around the cheekbones. Bending over to place her bag on the floor, she turned, looked at me, and sucked her teeth.

She wore big freeform dreadlocks that stood on top of her head in a messy bun. She plopped down on her bed and pulled out a rat tailed comb from the inside of her trousers. She unraveled her bun, and her waist length locs fell. She took the comb and dug from the root of her scalp, starting with the thick new growth that wasn't locked. She slid the comb down an inch until she reached the lock towards the middle of her hair strand and yanked it off. Although graceful by sight, I could feel and hear the pain of her hair being torn out of her head. She threw the strand in the middle of the cell between our two beds and repeated this process until three-quarters of her hair covered the entire floor. She didn't bother looking in my direction. She intently gazed at the wall in front of her and momentarily closed her eyes as she hummed to herself.

It wasn't until I stepped over the mess she'd made to reach the toilet that she spoke.

"How old is you, gal?"

Startled by the question because she didn't even know my name, I responded with sass and confusion.

"How old are you, ma'am?"

I don't care how old this bitch is but she not about to lil' girl me. I'm a grown ass woman.

"Doh bother 'bout mi age, gal. Ahs old and gray. But you. Yuhs ripe, gal. Yuhs still af a chance. Yuh af chillren?"

"I have one."

"Good, good. Yuh aff ah mon?"

"Maybe."

"Yuh eiffa aff a mon orr you don't."

I sat quiet and crouched over the toilet, getting ready to release. "Gal friend! Do you aff a mon?" she demanded.

I grabbed the toilet paper and wiped myself and remained quiet as the gushing sound of the toilet flushing washed out her voice.

"With all due respect, ma'am. Don't question me. Please and thank you."

A low chuckle came from her direction. Then, she followed it up with an emotionless sinister tri part laugh.

"Mi aff no more questions fah yuh gal friend, but listen so mi aff a warning fuh yuh! Never change yuhself, never change yuh makeup or yuh identity fuh a mon!"

As I walked over to my bed, she frantically jumped up from hers, standing barefoot on top of the locs she just yanked out of her head.

I stood frozen and gave her a piercing look, unaware of what she was capable of doing.

"Yuh hea mi gal?"

"Yeah, I hear you," I said sarcastically. "Listen, don't start the crazy shit, lady. I do not have time today."

"Look at mi! Yuh hea wah mi say? Neva eva change yuhself fuh a mon."

"Okay, I got it," I responded and went to sit down.

I noticed she was still standing as I turned around. Her eyes were bloodshot red and full of water. Her face was dark and hallow. She had both hands full with the locs she'd just yanked out of her head. She fell to her knees on top of the pile of hair and began banging on the floor.

"Neva! Yuh hea me! Neva! Listen to me! LISTEN TO ME! Neva! Yuh hea me, bitch? Do yuh hea the words coming out mi mouth? NEVA!"

She got louder and louder until she was screaming at the top of her lungs.

"NEVA. NEVA. YOU HEA ME? I SAID NEVA. LISTEN TO ME, BITCH! NEVA!"

Her voice carried throughout the cell block as she began to weep. The tears streamed down her face, and her weep escalated to a hackle. She blew her nose on her shirt while the stench grew stronger and now included her bad breath. I was shocked and afraid. I didn't know what to do. Still on her knees, she reached out and grabbed my foot. Startled, I looked down at her as she kneeled on all fours in desperation. With a daring twinkle in her eye, she looked like a true mad woman.

To my surprise, her touch was warm and welcoming. Not icky, grimy, or cold.

"Promise me, bitch, yuh won't eva change yaself fuh no mon."

My response time must have been too slow because she demanded again.

"Gal friend, listen hea. Listen to me; neva eva change..."

Before she could get out the rest of the sentence, she began to weep again. This time hysterically. Initially, I was motionless due to fear, but a tear rolled out of my eye once I glanced back at her face. I hopped off of the bed onto the floor and wrapped my arms around her. She unclenched her fists and let her hair fall from her hands.

She sat still and received my embrace, which intensified her crying as she buried her face in my shoulder. I patted her back and whispered in her ear. "Shh. Shh. Don't cry. I promise to neva change myself for a man." I repeated it three or four times and within seconds, she fell asleep in my arms. After struggling to lift her, I gave up and decided to place her pillow under her head and cover her with her blanket on the floor. For the next four hours, she slept, and I sat still, watching her intently— patiently waiting for visitation time to see Nia but impatiently waiting to go home.

CHAPTER 18

MANAGER

someone who controls resources and expenditures.

Nia walked into the visiting room wearing my sexy, white, form-fitting blouse and a tight pair of jeans. I was surprised to see her by herself. I thought Tony would have come in with her, but I guess it was best he let her come alone. She looked around aimlessly at the other inmates searching for me, her mother. I allowed her to look around a bit more before I called to her.

"Nia, baby, I'm over here."

She looked up excitedly with a big smile and shuffled between two guards and an inmate to get to me. I was so excited to see her. Her hair looked nice and healthy, in a short doobie. I embraced her tightly as soon as she got near and kissed her cheek.

"Hey, baby. You look so pretty. Who told you to wear my shirt, missy?" I said playfully. It was a white, long-sleeved V- neck jeweled blouse that accentuated Nia's cleavage. boxed out some of her cleavage. At twelve years old, Nia had full breasts. She was curvy and didn't have the kangaroo pouch I did, so the shirt fit her better than me. I couldn't be mad at her. She was due for some new clothes anyway.

"Hi, Mommy. I miss you," she said softly, looking up at me.

"Oh, baby, I miss you too. I miss you so much, sweetie. I'm so sorry." I released her from my embrace.

"Come, come, sit down," I said, motioning her over to the chairs.

The chipped, wooden table separated our chairs from each other. I sat down and reached for her hands while scanning the room with my peripherals. The visiting room was moderately busy. With less than ten inmates, there were at least fifteen COs scattered throughout the room.

I looked Nia right in the eyes.

"Baby. I promise you. No more," I said, shaking my head.

"I will be home before the school year is finished, baby, and I'm never coming here again. You'll never have to come here again. As soon as I'm done with my sentence, I'll be free and off of probation."

"I know, Mommy," she said as a tear rolled down the side of her face. Still leaned in, I released my right hand from hers and wiped her tear with my thumb.

"Baby, don't cry. I'm right here. I don't want you coming here, but if you want to see me, you can come as often as you want."

The sadness in her face broke my heart. To lighten the mood, I changed the subject.

"So, baby. How's school going? You should have gotten a progress report, right? How'd you do this period? Got an A again in English?"

She snatched her hand away from me, leaned back into the chair, and folded her arms.

"No. Can we talk about something else? Like exactly when are you coming home, Mommy?" she probed.

"Sometime in May. But as I asked, how were your grades this marking period?"

"I just told you I don't want to talk about it."

"Don't have me call up to that school and find out myself. Because I will."

Nia sucked her teeth. "Go ahead. Call them from jail. Auntie already seen my progress report," she said sarcastically.

In a flash, I reached over the table and yanked her hand until her body jerked forward and her face was two inches from mine. "Listen, little bitch. Watch your mouth. I may be in here now, and you may be at your aunt's house for now, but I am and will always be your mother, and what I say goes! Inside here and outside of here! Now do you understand me?"

Nia didn't flinch or say a word. I tightened my grip and her grimace stiffened as she boldly served me a scolding look.

"Do you hear me?"

She remained quiet and I released her from my grip. I had to relax. I couldn't let any of these COs see me. Thank God her shirt wasn't short sleeved. I would have bruised her arm for sure.

"I don't know why you think that because I'm in here, you can disrespect me. I'm putting an end to this now. You're not staying at Gloria's house. You will stay at our house under Tony's supervision. He will bring you to see me twice a week, and we gonna get to the bottom of this shit with your grades. So, bring your homework. The other two days, Tony will take you to see your grandmother. You are to come straight home after school. No stopping at Gloria's house. No hanging out in Brevoort and definitely not at Patience's house. These are the new rules. Do you understand me"?

"Yes," she whispered softly.

"Speak up, bitch. I can't hear you."

"YES!" she screamed angrily.

"Good."

I got up from my chair and motioned over to hers. I gave her a kiss on the cheek and patted her back.

"See you next week, baby," I whispered in Nia's ear.

I waved my hand to motion over a guard. "Send my daughter back to the waiting room so my husband can use the rest of my time."

* * *

CALLING Nia's teachers was the last thing on my mind. She just enrolled in junior high school two months ago in September. The school year hadn't even progressed enough for me to remember her teachers' names. All I knew was that she loved her English teacher and she got a 95 average for all of her classes on her first progress report. Although I realistically couldn't call her teachers, I still had to pull rank.

Her attitude was getting progressively worse. She had a slick mouth just like me and Glo. Go figure. We were the only women she'd been around. We were the only examples of womanhood for her to model, so of course she took after us. But I didn't care. I was the mother and she was the child. And I made the rules, not Gloria, so I had to remind her who ran the show.

I was so confident in the new rules I set that I had no doubt that Tony would look after her. He gladly accepted the responsibility, and I was so relieved.

I returned to my cell to find my cellmate organizing her books on the desk.

She looked like she had showered and washed her hair. Her face appeared two to three shades lighter and brighter. The stench that filled the cell yesterday was practically gone. All I smelled was a light, airy musk. She was humming softly to herself and quickly stopped as soon as she noticed my presence. She was rather chipper when she saw me.

"Hey, gal. How yuh mon and daughta doing?" She turned from her desk, stopped playing with her books, and looked up at me.

I still didn't even know this woman's name and she didn't know mine either. She knew I had visitors when I lined up for the visitation line, but I never disclosed who was coming to see me. She just assumed I had a man and that he visited. I chuckled before I answered. I wasn't comfortable with her questioning me, but I was relieved that she appeared to be less disturbed.

I took a deep breath before saying, "My daughter is doing okay. Just had to lay down the new rules. Make sure she still knows who's boss, you know?"

"And yuh mon? How he so?"

"He's been stepping up. I'm grateful for him."

"Stepping up or overstepping, gal? Yuh mus know di difference between a mon and ah manager." She sucked her teeth so hard, it made a hissing sound.

"Trust me. I know. I'm good in that department."

"Yuh no shit gal! Tek time. Yuh soon learn. Listen to mi! Mi no whet it lik fuh be wid a mon yuh really af no business wid. Mi kno. Mi kno personally. Mi should af left mi mon from long time. Pree wah mi ah say. If he tell yuh wah to wear, how to comb an style yuh hair. If he make yuh change yuh clothes don't like the cuitex on yuh toes. If he ask yuh wea yuh been, weh time yuh go and yuh come in — there is something yuh need tuh kno, gal yuh don't af a mon, gal yuh af a manager."

She spoke so fast and soft; it sounded like a sweet song.

"Mi know. Cus mi ad a manager myself," she said before declaratively patting her chest. "And he manage mi til he nah wan fi manage mi no more. Then he let mi go just like that," she snapped her fingers. "Like a minimum wage job. Gone."

I was still exhausted from last night's emotional roller coaster with this woman that I lacked the energy and patience to endure one more night of her bullshit. I tried to show compassion. But first, I needed some understanding.

"What's your name, ma'am?" I asked.

"Don't bother about mi name, gal. Mi story is more important. I was a married woman fuh forty-tree years and mi af nuttin fuh show fuh it. No chillren, no education, no family, barely any friends. And now mi af no husband. All these years mi been faithful to only him and his vision of mi life, mi style, how I wea mi hair, wea mi clothes, wea mi eat. Mi whole life, I became who mi man wan mi fuh be. Not who mi wan fuh be. Mi tought if mi do wah, he ask he would never leave me. In di end, mi still wind up alone." She shrugged her shoulders and shook her head.

"Mi ah jus thank God fuh mi life."

CHAPTER 19

EGO

your idea or opinion of yourself, especially your feeling of your own importance and ability

I barely slept. As the night went on, I grew more and more anxious sharing a cell with this woman. Although seeing Nia did put me at ease, it was only momentarily. I was now worried about Pam. It was almost two weeks since I last saw her, and I hadn't spoken to Gloria in a few days. I refused to call Glo and kiss her ass again. I had to get in touch with the nursing home myself.

The next morning, I headed to the law library. The librarian was an older, Jewish man who was rather chipper. I had never seen him here. He had to be new because he was rather polite and welcoming. It was clear that the corruption of the job hadn't seeped into him yet, and I planned to be long gone before it did.

"Hi. I need to find the numbers to the Cobble Hill Patient Facility in Brooklyn, New York. My mother is a patient there," I said sweetly.

I learned a long time ago that you win more bees with honey, not only in life but definitely in jail as well. If you wanted something from someone, having an attitude wasn't gonna get it.

"Sure. Sure. Hold on," he said as he typed furiously on his keyboard. The strokes on the keyboard were so loud, the sound screeched my eardrums.

"Hmm." He lowered his glasses and leaned forward towards the monitor.

"There looks like there are different numbers. Do you know what department she's in? That may help you locate her faster."

"She's on dialysis and she's doing physical therapy."

The librarian slapped his hand on the computer mouse and anxiously moved it back and forth. After a few minutes, he finally shouted, "Got it."

He picked up a pen and scribbled some numbers on a yellow post it and handed it to me.

"Here. There are three numbers. The first is the main line, the second is for the Dialysis Unit, and the last number is for the Physical Therapy Ward. Hope this helps."

"Thank you so much."

The librarian was so accommodating and swift that I had enough time to make three phone calls. I could call two of the numbers he gave me and Tony.

The first call I made was to the nursing patient unit. It rang for about two minutes before I just hung up. Thinking about Pam's condition on top of being away from her at such a crucial time saddened and angered me all at once. Pam was my only friend. The only person who wouldn't judge me. The only person who could say something in this instance to make me laugh. Struggling to get in contact with her grieved my heart. I needed to know that I would reach her when I called.

Exhausted, I tried dialing Tony's number just to check in on Nia and take my mind off of Pam momentarily. After six rings, it went to voicemail, which was odd because Tony usually answered his phone on the first or second ring. I had one call left. I could possibly sneak in a fourth. I turned around to see which correctional officers were there.

Yeah, it wasn't happening. Maybe on the next call block.

I had to think quick. Should I call Tony, or should I call Glo? Eeny, meeny, miny, moe.

After the seventh ring, Gloria finally answered the phone.

"Yes, Joi-Ann?" Gloria asked annoyingly.

"Gloria, I been tryna get in touch with you for days. I had to have Tony bring Nia to visit me so I could talk to my daughter 'cause you haven't been answering the phone. How's Pam?"

"This is what you constantly have fucked up. The world does not revolve around you, Joi. I'm dealing with shit too. I have my own shit. My own son. Now, I got Pam and her shit on top of dealing with your shit. So, don't call my phone questioning me about anything."

"Glo, I'm just tryna figure out what's going on. Why can't we talk and handle things in a civilized manner?"

She chuckled, and it turned into a long laugh.

"What the fuck is so funny, Gloria?"

"You. You're funny. So where was the civil conversation before you had some strange man go pick up my niece from school and take her all the way to Rikers Island without my knowledge? Joi, you're full of shit, yet you think you're so fucking smart."

"Gloria, I couldn't get in touch with you for two days! Last time we spoke, you had my daughter staying out 'til damn near midnight. That shit ain't flying with me at all."

"And neither is this new man of yours. You allowing him to overstep like he's her fucking stepfather. That ain't ya man. That's somebody's else husband. Nia is my blood, and I ain't having her staying in no house with some strange man."

"Gloria Maxine, you better pipe down. Nia is my daughter, in case you haven't recognized, and we have a great arrangement set up. Tony's going to bring her to visit me twice a week. The other two days, I was going to have Tony take her to the nursing home. Since you not driving, I can have Tony take all of you to go see Pam."

"See, here you go. Thinking you better than someone. I would love to take him up on his offer to drive us to see Pam, but I don't want to ride in no car with no stink ass Jamaican. Now as soon as I get ahold of my niece, I'll make sure she sees Pam, most likely more than twice a week, but if I gotta bring her ass to Rikers, it ain't happening. So, would you like to have a civil conversation now about how you're going to see your daughter?"

"Glo, I don't need you to step in this time. I got this. Don't worry. I trust him. You just do what you're asked of — your auntie duties and nothing more. Nia has a mother, and it's not you. Don't you forget it."

"And don't you forget where you're at. Watch your tone on this recorded line, bitch," she sneered before I heard a loud slam and dial tone on the other end of the phone.

* * *

I WAS DETERMINED to get through to Pam. I was hoping she could talk some sense into Gloria. I knew Pam would not agree to Glo not bringing Nia to see me. Either way, I needed to speak to her. I needed to know how she was doing. I was also her legal proxy, so only I could make really important decisions on her behalf.

Gloria was talking all big and bold, but in fact, she was nothing more than a runner. She ran errands and handled all the busy work — dialysis, food shopping, etc., which was why she'd been overwhelmed. But it was time for her to know what it was like to get up every day and tend to a list of responsibilities. She tried to call the shots because I was in here but we both knew who really made the decisions.

My role as a big sister taught me early on about the power of coaxing your inferior's ego to get what you wanted. I knew that as long as I let Glo think she had the control, I could avoid miscommunication and arguments and I would ultimately get what I wanted. Men used this all the time on women by calling us beautiful, complimenting us, and making us smile and blush. Making us so desperately believe in their adoration of us more than our own belief of what we're worth. They were able to get what they wanted from us even if they didn't truly adore us.

Not many women knew how to employ this very same tactic, but it was my gift. I coaxed Clyde's ego, and he took care of me and my daughter for eleven years. Clyde felt good just being with me. Even though he was an idiot, he loved how smart and motivating I was. Although he would never rise to the occasion, I always showered him with affirmations and told him he could get a job and keep it if he ever really stopped hustling. My affirmations never made him get a job, but it made him hustle harder.

Tony was no exception. I made him feel smart, strong, and undefeated. I reassured him of his strength whenever he shared experiences about his very humble upbringing. I knew how to get my needs met by the men I dealt with. That was the difference between me and Gloria, and she was always jealous of that as we got older. Yeah, she was cuter. But her cuteness was a waste. None of the men she dealt with ever took her seriously. She never had a serious relationship or a live-in man. For years, she would always say she never wanted a man because she enjoyed her freedom, but I knew deep down inside that she wished she had a partner in crime, someone other than her sister or her mother she could call when things went south.

She hated the fact that I always had a man who would go above and beyond to make me happy. That was why she made those comments about him. Jealous bitch. But I wasn't worried. I knew that as soon as I spoke to Pam, she would help straighten Gloria out as she always did.

* * *

"First name is Pamela, last name is HOLLOWAY. H-O-L-L-O-W-A-Y. This is her daughter, Joyce-Ann."

"Hold please," whined the woman administrator who answered. As I stood nervously, awaiting someone to resume the call, I twirled up the phone wire with my index finger. I looked down at the floor and saw a shadow of my face and the six inmates lined up behind me to make calls.

After thirty seconds, someone picked up the phone.

"Hi, Ms. Holloway. This is Nurse Denton. How can I help you?

"I am calling to speak with my mother, Pamela Holloway. She is a PT rehab and dialysis patient. I called the nursing patient line earlier and it rang out."

"I apologize about that. Your mother is my patient. She is actually seeing the doctor at this moment. Do you have a call back number so I can have her return your call when she's finished with the doctor?"

"No ma'am, I do not have a call back number. I can just call back. Actually, I am her legal proxy, and I am out of town on business until about May. Could I join in on this appointment via phone? Can I speak with the doctor?"

"Unfortunately, something like that would have to be approved prior to the day of the appointment. What is your first name again, Ms. Holloway?

"Joyce-Ann."

"Give me a second while I pull up your mom's file."

I heard typing on the keyboard and the shuffling of papers. I looked down at my wrist, only to remember I didn't have a watch and couldn't tell the time. I didn't want the nurse to hear the corrections warning, "you have 120 seconds left on this phone call."

"Repeat your first name again."

"Joyce-Ann," I repeated in irritation.

"No, that's not what I see here. I have a Gloria Maxine Holloway down as the legal proxy. When you said legal proxy and that you were out of town, I was confused because Gloria was just here last night with her son and daughter to see your mother."

"Ma'am, that's not correct. During my mother's first appointment, I signed documentation to be appointed as the legal proxy. We had a lawyer from the nursing home witness me sign the documentation."

"Give me a second, Ms. Holloway."

I heard more keyboard clicks. Then, a brief moment of silence before she let out a loud, "Hmm."

"Ms. Holloway, it looks like two days ago, your mother signed over your rights to your sister. With that being said, I cannot discuss any of your mother's medical history with you. I actually shared too much already. I will notify your mother that you called, and if you leave a call back number, I will have her return your call. If not, you are free to call back before seven pm."

CHAPTER 20

DEFERENCE

humble submission or respect

For the first time in my life, I felt alone. Despite how many times I got arrested or how many times I survived a shootout, I knew I always had Pam. I knew Pam was always a call away. I knew her home was always open to me, and most importantly, she was the only person in the world who would never judge me. She was the only person in the world who I knew loved me unconditionally.

I missed her so much and just wanted to hear her voice. Everything was happening so fast and it just wouldn't stop. Every day in jail progressively got worse. I felt like I was losing control of my life. I was losing my daughter. I was losing my mother. I was losing my man and my sister. I was almost certain I lost my job, but that was of no concern to me. Lose one job, get another one. You can't adopt that motto to your loved ones. No one spirit ever replaces another. Each one is unique.

You can get another friend, another man, or even another child, but you will never have another mother. The objective is to cherish your mom while she's here. Although I'd been there with Pam through everything —drug addiction, domestic violence, and extreme poverty, I felt awful knowing that I couldn't be there for her while battling Hepatitis C. Gloria complained about tending to Pam, but if I had the luxury to and didn't have to work, I would have gladly been there.

The timing was just horrible, and the communication between Glo and I was not improving. Glo overstepped her boundaries out of spite, not for genuine concern for Nia's wellbeing. She was trying to take my baby away from me and turn her against me. I could see her scheme from a mile ahead, but I refused to give it life. Sometimes you have to treat people with unexpected kindness in the midst of their schemes.

I was well aware that I was walking on eggshells and needed to tip toe around very lightly. It seemed like no matter how hard I tried to have a decent conversation with Glo, it always went left. I could apologize to her, and she would still find a bone to pick with me. Nothing had changed since we were younger. Glo always hated me and whenever she had the chance to spite me, she did. It would have actually shocked me if she didn't try.

Her behavior was totally expected. In fact, it was a tad bit too predictable. I had to show her different. I couldn't be predictable, which was why I just brushed off her threat about getting ahold of Nia. Although I wasn't worried, I was livid at her audacity.

Literally starving, I made my way to the cafeteria after I hung up the phone. I was hungry and needed some real sustenance. Cookies, chips, and soup just weren't going to do it. I needed a sandwich. Peanut butter & jelly or turkey and cheese would do. I'd even take tuna or ham, but I didn't want any sugary snacks.

After getting my tray with two sandwiches and about five cartons of cup-sized apple juice, I scurried past the lunch tables that were full and sat at an empty one. I took one bite into my ham and cheese, and it literally was the best thing I'd eaten in days. The apple juice was a great follow-up to the sandwich as well.

I spent the last bit of money Tony put on my books yesterday. I racked up on some soup, snacks, and some hygiene products like soap and shaving razors. I was in need of some more funds. I had some money in the bank and was going to need Tony to retrieve it from the ATM for me. Too bad I couldn't get my own sister to do it for me and had to rely on a man I'd just recently met.

Throughout the entire time that I'd been locked up, Gloria had made it difficult to talk to her. Glo might have picked a bone in the past with me, but she never got in between Me and Nia. When I was pregnant with Nia during my first bid, Gloria was the best sister I could have asked for. She was there for me. She showed up and she was glad to.

My most recent bid before now, Nia stayed with Pam at her apartment. Glo was also instrumental and helpful in making sure Nia got to school, got new clothes, and stayed out of trouble. Glo may have talked about me like a dog in front Nia and shamed me for my crimes, but she didn't condone Nia being outside late. She was actually stricter with Nia in comparison to her son.

So, what had changed? Was it just because Nia was no longer a virgin? Was it because I was locked up and she wanted to spite me? Was it because she was overwhelmed? I wasn't sure and it didn't matter; I just needed a game plan. I had to get in touch with Pam and Tony.

I looked up from the lunch tray after taking the last bite of my sandwich. I guzzled down all five of the apple juice cartons and proceeded to walk over to the trash can, but I was stopped by my cellmate, who I hadn't seen since the morning. She wore her hair in a low ponytail while her new growth stuck out. All of her locs were completely combed out. I guess she finally got around to finishing it.

"Yuh eat-tin dis slop, galfriend?" she asked inquisitively as she quickly fluttered her wild eyes open and shut while facing me.

"When you hungry, you'd be surprised what you'd eat."

"Not ah a day in hell. Mi nuh eat meat noway, no suh."

* * *

Recreation time in jail usually consisted of at least sixty inmates outside fighting the wind with their chestnut bomber jackets that the facility loaned them. When it was winter, it was always cold. If the cold was unbearable, they wouldn't let us out, but today's weather wasn't too bad. The sun was high in the sky and although the wind was still present, the heat from the sun did us some justice.

During rec time, you got acquainted with the rest of the inmates. You got to see everyone. The possibility of running into someone you knew from the outside was more likely during rec time than any other time, which was why I normally rejected my rec time and headed for the cell. But today, I needed some fresh air to think.

I wondered if Gloria was going to force my hand and try to intervene to get Nia. I didn't want to mention it to Tony because I didn't want to alarm him. I also didn't want him to be worried. I couldn't flat-out tell him that my decision to make him Nia's caregiver was causing family drama. I didn't want him to know all the details about the issues with me and Glo. Although he knew I chose to rely on him, he didn't have to know the intricate details of why I made that decision. The last thing you want is a man to think you have no family. If he was a predator, he could take advantage of that vulnerability and use it.

Luckily, I didn't really have to worry about him using anything against me because he'd been nothing but good to me. He'd been showing up. He brought Nia here and now, he was looking after her. Telling him about the family drama this decision stirred up would turn him off and maybe even sadden him which were not my intentions at all. I wanted him to know how grateful I was for him. I wanted him to know how much of a help he'd been, and I knew filling him in on the extras with Gloria was unnecessary.

I stepped out into the yard full of green grass, cornered by barbed-wire gates that were at least twenty-five feet tall. There were women all scattered around, mainly ganged up in groups, yet some lingered by their lonesome. The groups varied by race primarily, then by addiction. One thing was for sure, drugs didn't discriminate. A crack or heroin addiction could make a Jew and a KKK Klansman best of friends. Although we lived in a world where they would normally hate each other, in prison, they were bonded by their demons.

There was the crack crew, the dope fiends, the middle class, rich cokeheads and so on. The meth crew was probably the least racially diverse. Tucked in the far-right corner were mainly young white girls with gruesome red pimples on their faces and broken light bulb pieces for teeth. If the racial makeup of the meth crew differed, let's just say the color of their skin didn't. There could have been a few Hispanic girls sprinkled in their circle, but from the color of their skin you couldn't tell the difference between them and their white peers.

I spotted an empty space near the gate where the black crew congregated. As a black woman from the projects in Brooklyn, there was no other group more fitting. I said hello, addressing everyone and stood a bit off to the side but still near them. I wanted my body language to convey exactly what I intended, which was respect and deference. Deference went a long way in jail. It saved you from a lot of harm. If you were lucky, you'd learn this lesson your first three months in prison. If you were teachable, you'd learn how to implement it within your first three months.

I was nineteen years old and pregnant my first time in jail, so I learned early on about deference — both sides — giving deference and receiving it. My pregnancy granted me some deference from correction officers and other inmates. Generally, most people respected the birth of children and infants, which extended to me in being pregnant. As soon as I gave birth, my deference began to dwindle away. The other times I returned to prison in my twenties and without child, I got used to giving deference instead of receiving it. It saved my life many times and made sentences easier to complete.

With my back pressed against the gate, all I could think about was, *how could Pam allow Gloria to remove me as her legal proxy without even speaking to me first?* She hadn't even heard from me since I got locked up. How could she condone that decision? I was relying on Pam to neutralize the situation between Glo and me. To know that Pam was on her side disappointed me.

I was abruptly interrupted from my sulking thoughts by a nudge in my side. I blinked once and as soon as my vision got clearer, I saw my cellmate standing beside me.

"Gal, yuh mus be daydreamin' or wah, mi ah call pon you a few times."

"Yeah, I was. Thanks for interrupting."

"Yuh know, mi still think about how yuh nuh tell mi bout tis mon of yous."

"Because it's none of your fucking business. Damn, woman. Why are you so pressed about my man? Damn!"

I was starting to get upset. She just wouldn't let it go.

"Listen, gal. Mi try fuh warn yuh. Fuh sum reason, mi ah feel lik yuh af a Rasta mon. Like mi mon."

Wait. Wait. Wait. How the fuck did she know that? Was she stalking me? I looked at her again and for a split second, I questioned if she resembled the woman I saw in the market back in Jamaica talking to Tony.

Nah. It wasn't her. She was too light. The woman in the market was at least four shades darker than my cellmate. I played it cool before responding.

"How you figure that?"

"Mi nuh kno. Mi just figure. Mi could be wrong. It could be all in mi head. Lik mi say, mi wah fuh save yuh, gal, so mi hope mi story could be an inspiration tuh yuh."

The more she talked, the more pronounced her musk became. Her body movements revealed the smell I remembered from our first night in the cell together. A combination of funk, musk, and fish smacked me in the face. I turned to the right and noticed the crew of black women I initially stood near had moved about twenty feet away from us. Although moderate, thank God the wind was strong enough to break down her repulsive smell, making it bearable enough that I didn't have to cover my nose.

Fed up with the mysterious bullshit, I confronted her.

"I don't want to hear shit from you if I can't know yuh name gal friend," I mocked her favorite line.

"Ora. Mi name is Ora, gal, which means prayer, and mi need one bad yuh hea so. Mi nuh kno how long mi fuh be hea inna dis jail. Dem judge af evidence pon mi. Dem say mi kill mi husband."

She paused and then chuckled.

"Mi nuh know who kill he, but him deserve every lick he get. Mi jus doh know how judge fuh pin pon me," she wept disappointedly.

* * *

LATER ON, in the cell, I sat and watched Ora spray herself with homemade mint water in hopes of masking her strong odor. It was a huge disappointment — not because it didn't work, but more so because she knew it didn't work and attempted to spray herself every fifteen minutes.

As soon as I was about to take a nap to drown out her presence and smell, I heard a loud bang on my cell door.

"Holloway. Up. You have a visitor."

I was shocked. I wasn't expecting anyone. Pam was sick and Glo already made it known that she wasn't coming to see me at all. I hadn't spoken to Tony since he brought Nia up here two days ago, so he was the last person I expected. I jumped up and slipped into my house slippers. The guard handcuffed me and walked me out of the cell. He escorted me through the jail, out to the visiting area, which was ten times brighter than the cell block.

When we reached the entrance of the visiting room, I rubbed my hands together out of nervousness.

Who could it be?

The doors slid open, and I stepped into the visiting area. The guard escorted me to my table and uncuffed me. I sat patiently, this time diagonal from the last seat I was in when Nia visited.

After ten minutes of twiddling my thumbs, the pinging sound rang, singling the new influx of visitors. The door slid open, and eight people walked forward. Amongst them stood Tony. He was looking good too. His visit was unexpected but much needed and wanted. It looked like he was dressed up like the many times he came to pick me up from my apartment for dinner. He was rocking a Coogi outfit head to toe. The sweater was red and green with a bold, elaborate print design. His jeans were mainly blue with small accents of red and green, and he sported a pair of Jordans with them. Although he couldn't wear it inside the visiting area, I was almost certain he wore his red Kangol hat to complement the look.

Seeing him look good made me feel good. My face lit up with joy as soon as we made eye contact. He forced a half smirk as he walked over to me. When he approached me, I leaned in for a passionate peck and some tongue, but he dodged my lips, so my kiss was planted on his cheek. I was instantly offended but tried to hide it.

"Hey, baby. Thanks for coming to see me looking all good. An unexpected, pleasant surprise."

"Babygal. Mi like yuh, mi really do but tis ting wid yuh is getting rel complicated. At first, mi nuh worry bcus it no burden pon me fuh look pon yuh daughta. Mi haf two daughtas of mi own. Mi nuh pedophile so mi nuh worry. Mi kno wah fuh do. But mi ah get a visit pon mi job today from ah detective tawkin bout ah order of protection against a Gloria Holloway. At first mi nuh even know who it is. Then mi tink, oh Joi last name is Holloway. Must be she sister and mi right."

He deepened his voice but lowered his tone and looked me boldly in the eyes.

"Joi. Mi nuh af time fuh lock up wid police. Mi nuh cum dis country fuh wrestle wid police ova pickney dat nuh even mine. Yuh need fuh check yuhself. Real bod, gal. Mi nuh do yuh nuttin fuh yuh sister fuh give mi name tuh police. Mi ah just be hea fuh yuh wid no complaints. Dis ting hea getting' too much fuh me tuh handle. Mi ah tink it's best for yuh daughta tuh go by she tante. Yesterday, mi nuh answer none of yuh calls bcus mi nuh kno how fuh tell yuh Nia nuh come home all last night, but mi bet tree bloodclot thousand U.S. dollars, she went pon yuh sista house, and that's wea she need fuh stay. Mi af fuh come talk tuh yuh face to face. Mi put five hundred dollas pon yuh books, darling. Get yuh head together and only call mi if yuh need something, but mi come back hea unless it's to take yuh home."

He leaned over and gave me a light peck on the lips and motioned over the guard. As the guard approached, he instantly stood up and turned his back to me. I watched the words "Coogi" spelled in all white lettering fade away as he disappeared behind the sliding door to be escorted back downstairs to the holding area to go home.

CHAPTER 21

INSOMNIA

a sleep disorder in which you have trouble falling and/or staying asleep, difficulty going into a subconscious place, easily distracted and unable to block out conflicting elements around oneself.

Insomnia hit me hard like an eighteen-wheeler truck. I couldn't sleep. I refused to sleep. I paced back and forth the entire night. Ora stayed up with me for a while and just yelled obscenities, thinking she was helping by uniting in my frustration, but she wasn't helping at all. She couldn't help because she didn't know what was going on, and I wasn't sharing. It took too much to process what had just happened to even express it, especially to a stranger.

By the time Tony left the jail, I missed the opportunity to make a phone call. I couldn't believe Gloria went as far as filing an order of protection against a man who never harmed her. The hate Glo had for me ran deep. She just wanted to spite me.

She didn't care about Nia. If she cared about my daughter, she wouldn't have been letting her run wild, taking her to the doctor behind my back, letting her stay out late, and all of that shit.

There was no unity amongst us. She would pair up with a child to fight against me rather than upholding what was right and what was in the best interest of the child. Frankly, I had no problem with Nia staying with Gloria if she ran a tighter ship. Glo knew what it was like to be a young girl growing up in Brooklyn, especially the projects, and she didn't seem concerned at all with protecting her baby niece. As older women in the family, we had to protect our girls and not enable the toxic normalities we'd experienced or grown accustomed to. It was our responsibility to hold Nia to a higher standard.

It was never my intention to maliciously involve Tony. He was just available at a time that I really needed a hand and a friend, and I couldn't rely on my sister to be there. I only had one call. One chance. So, I made a choice. And I thought including Gloria in the plans would get her on board, but I was sadly mistaken.

She was making it very hard for me to trust and respect her. I was on guard, and it sucked because I was alone. The one person who'd been here for me since I got locked up just put me on pause. First, he was rocking with me, but as soon as I became a burden, he changed how we rocked; more so, he changed how he rocked with me.

My mother wasn't available, and my sister and daughter formed an alliance against me. Tony was right. More than likely, Nia was at Gloria's house, so I wasn't worried for her safety. I wasn't under the impression that my daughter was missing, but I still needed to speak to her. If the arrangement was for Nia to stay with Glo for the rest of this measly bid, we had to establish some rules and boundaries.

And it had to be done quickly. I stayed up all night, anticipating the sunlight to make my first call for the morning. I didn't brush my teeth or wash my face. Those were the least of my concerns. I headed straight to the commissary and bought a pack of Newport Shorts. The nicotine took a bit of the edge off.

I headed outside for the morning rec time and made my way to the first person I saw with a lighter. She was a white, young cokehead. Her teeth were so white it looked like she didn't smoke a cigarette a day in her life. You could tell she came from money. Looked like mob money. She passed the lighter, and I lit my cigarette and took a deep pull. I passed the lighter back to her, nodded my head to say thank you, and walked to the other side.

This was the worst time for all of this shit to be happening. This was the first time I was really alone inside. Although Clyde wasn't shit, he was there, he was loyal, and he was a rider. He never backed down to Gloria. Gloria always hated him 'cause he wasn't no sucker. She would call Clyde all kinds of creepy, freaky crackheads.

I'm not glorifying the toxicity of me and Clyde's relationship but I knew I could count on him. I knew he wasn't afraid of no police, and I knew he would do some time for me if it meant I could be home with Nia. Why? Because he did it before.

We caught a few cases getting money together where Clyde had to do a bid or two — four months, six months, and the most, fourteen months, but I held it down. And when I got locked up last time, he held it down for Nia also.

Nia did sleep at Pam's house, but Clyde was instrumental in bringing her to see me, taking her shopping and to school, and ultimately, coordinating with Pam to make things happen. I needed a nigga like Clyde right about now to hold down the fort. On the flipside, I couldn't be mad at Tony. Clyde was my man-man. Tony and I were just really locking in. The truth was, we both were coming into this shit with some demons — him being married and my run-ins with the law. Our honeymoon phase was over. We were naked. We were raw, and we saw each other's complexities. He did what he knew best to do. He provided and stepped back, and I couldn't be mad at that. He wasn't Clyde. He was a different kind of man.

I put out my cigarette, dropped it to the grassy ground, and stubbed it with the ball of my shoe. It was time to face Glo and Nia, and come to some kind of understanding. I headed to the phone booth area and quickly punched in Glo's cell phone number. She didn't answer. I hung up and dialed her house phone, and it rang off the hook.

Fed up, I dialed the nursing wing at Pam's nursing home. After a few moments, a male voice answered the phone.

"How may I direct your call?"

"I'm calling to speak with Nurse Denton. This is Joi-Ann Holloway, Pam Holloway's daughter."

"Oh, I know Pam. Such a sweet, feisty lady. Are you the sister that's incarcerated? Your mom and sister talk about you all the time."

I was in disbelief. Were these bitches really up in this nursing home telling my business?

"Nah, that's my other sister. May I speak with my mother, please?"

"Oh. I'm so sorry. Sure. Give me a second."

I waited on the phone for about three minutes before I heard a voice on the other end. The shuffling of the phone rattled in my ear as I waited for someone to address me.

"Here you go, Pam. It's your daughter, Joi," I heard vaguely in the background.

"Joi. Oh, my baby girl. How are you doing, Sista Suki?"

"Ma. I don't even know where to begin. I haven't spoken to you in so long it feels. But I got caught up on some probation shit. Then, Gloria is moving real funny with me and had Nia staying out at all times of night on a school day. Then, she ain't been keeping me in the loop about you at all. Shit just crazy, ma."

"Baby girl, just hold ya head. This bid will be done soon. You'll soon be home and things will be back to normal. You could come see me 'cause I sure miss you. It's nice seeing my grand baby. Gloria brings her every other day. She's getting so pretty and big. My girls — Joi, Gloria & Nia," she said cheerfully.

"Ma, I miss you too. But what's going on? Why did you let Gloria remove me as your legal proxy? Now I can't call the nursing home and talk to your doctors. And why y'all telling these fucking people my business? They don't need to know I'm in jail. You got this male fucking nurse asking me am I the one incarcerated. What the fuck, ma?" I yelled.

"Joi, baby girl, you not gon' be calling here yelling and screaming at me. Okay? I don't know what you're talking about. Gloria told me you guys agreed that was the best decision. So, I went along with it. I hadn't spoken to you."

"That's because I couldn't get in touch with you. Gloria was not answering the phone for days. I didn't even speak to my daughter on the phone. I had to have Tony come bring her to visit me just to speak to her. I still haven't spoken to Nia on the phone yet. Every time I call Gloria to handle some real business, she be on some bullshit, and it go left."

"Joi, you know your sister. You always been the more responsible one, so you gotta take the high road. Don't argue with Gloria. Play nice to get what you need. Remember, self-preservation comes first. You know that. You ain't new to this. You been here before. Do your time like a big girl, Sista Suki. But trust me, I been talking to your sister, knocking some sense into her 'cause she was talking about seeking custody of Nia and I had to laugh. 'Glo you can't be serious. Your son can't even read a full paragraph out loud,' I told her. Joi, you of all people know your sister is crazy," she said jokingly.

"Custody? Of who? My daughter? That bitch really crazy. Yeah, you better check your daughter, Pam, 'cause I'm not having that shit. Who the fuck she think she is?"

"Slow yo' roll, baby girl, remember to check yaself when talking to me. You may be grown, but I'm still ya momma," Pam replied snappily.

"Nah, fuck that, Pam. That bitch got some nerve. Fuck is wrong with her?"

"Joi-Ann. I got dialysis at 3pm. I'm 'bout to relax until then. You take care of yaself, baby girl."

She made a smooching sound with her lips before saying, "Ciao" and hanging up the phone.

CHAPTER 22

PATIENCE

the capacity to accept or tolerate delay, trouble, or suffering without getting angry or upset. Having patience means you can remain calm, even when you've been waiting forever or dealing with something painstakingly slow.

I returned to my cell with mixed emotions. It felt good talking to Pam, but I hated when she hung up on me — especially in jail. It hit me hard because I couldn't call back. I think the worst thing to do to a person in jail is hang up on them. Those few calls we get a day are our lifeline to sanity and to the outside world.

People take advantage of basic privileges when they know you're locked down on the inside and need them. Pam knew I was going crazy not being able to speak to her. The worst of it all was that I still didn't even know how she was really doing. It seemed like Glo was determined to cut me out of everything. She didn't want me to be involved with Pam's care, yet when I was home, she barely wanted to step up. Now she was trying to take custody of my daughter. I wasn't having that. This had just gone too far.

I wish I had someone to talk to. When I was in jail with Nia, group counseling really worked. Those sessions that taught me a lot about life as a pregnant teenage girl with a crackhead mother. The women in the group were older and had really broken lives. Their stories inspired me to push on because it gave me hope. In comparison to their stories, I had it good.

I made up my mind in those sessions to come home and turn my life around for Nia. Although I was working and going to school for the most part, trying to live a straight life, the influence of Clyde's stinkin' thinking rubbed off on me, and we always found a way to survive — usually illegally.

My motto had always been one foot in, and one foot out. As soon as I came home at twenty-one years old with a toddler, I made the decision to get out of the streets. I wasn't opposed to a little side money, but I refused to dedicate my life to crime because the cost of losing my daughter again was too expensive, and I simply could not afford it.

I reached for the box of Oreos I bought from commissary and chomped down four cookies. I was interrupted by my cellmate, who heard me smacking and licking my fingers.

"Gal, yuh gwan git big like ah house yuh keep eat-tin lik suh."

I ignored her. I didn't have time for her shit.

"Ain't yuh learn yuh can't avoid mi? Wah type of depression is yuh facing, gal? Yuh sentence soon dun."

"Depression? I don't get depressed. I go through shit. I brush it off and keep it pushing. This just how I cope. We all cope differently," I responded.

"Yaa fuh sure," she mumbled back.

"Where I come from, daily life can be depressing. To make it, you gotta just keep it pushing."

"So, whet gwan, gal?"

"Everything just falling apart. My mom's is sick in the nursing home. Me and my sister is at it, and she got my daughter running wild. Shit just not going right."

"It jail. Shit nuh go right fuh mi, she, she and he. Yuh nuh different gal. We all gwan tru. Yuh understand?"

"Everyone got a story, but why ask me if you not gon' listen?"

"Yuh rite, yuh brite. Gwan gal, tawk suh."

"Just forget it," I sighed.

I SHOULD HAVE NEVER SHARED anything with this woman. Simply because I still didn't know whether or not she was mentally sane. With all I had going on, finding out the status of her mental health was the least of my concerns. As long as she ain't overstep, we were good. One thing was for sure, I wasn't scared of no crackhead or lunatic. Whether in the streets or in jail, if I had to hold my own, I would. And if Ms. Ora got too out of hand, she would soon learn.

"No problem, gal. Yuh nuh need fuh talk, just listen. Be thankful and grateful fuh life. Yuh af a child, yuh af a mon, and yuh look like a smart enough gal tuh af a decent job. Don't worry, gal. Yuh nuttin' lik mi, so yuh win already. Time soon come and yuh be back home. Patience is key, gal."

The audacity of this woman to mention patience. I'd been in here almost a week and been keeping it together for the most part. She was the one throwing temper tantrums, not bathing or wearing deodorant, yet trying to teach me about patience.

"With all due respect, Ora, trust me, I know all about patience," I responded sarcastically.

"Shit! Yuh dumb dumb daym dumb and nuh kno nut-tin'. Yuh tink yuh better than mi, gal? Yuh tink yuh kno more 'bout life than mi? Mi see sixty-four years pon dis earth, galfriend. Mi kno more than yuh tink."

I remained quiet because the last thing I was going to do was argue with a deranged woman who yanked her hair out of her head for fun. I was just fed up with being here. I tried to be a good sport. I tried to remain positive despite blow after blow. I tried to remain calm, which was incredibly hard behind bars without marijuana.

All I could think about was smoking a nice jay and how it would ease the confusion and pain I was experiencing. One inhale of THC would put my mind at ease, and I so desperately needed that. The light buzz from the nicotine of a cigarette had nothing on a perfectly rolled spliff. Tony introduced me to that word. The first time he said, "bun a spliff," I was so confused.

"Bun a what?" I asked.

"A spliff? Roll sum weed, gal," he said.

"Oh, that's what you mean?" I asked dumbfounded and started crushing up some weed on a laminated 4x6 postcard in his car. I snapped out of daydream land and turned to face Ora.

"Ora, I don't have time for your madness today. Please just leave me alone," I said in a spirit of defeat.

I really just wanted some peace and silence. I didn't want to hear her voice, and I didn't even want to hear my thoughts. I just wanted to eat, drink, smoke, and sleep. If I could spend the rest of my sentence without speaking to Ora, I would gladly be delighted. If she could be moved to a different cell, I would be ecstatic, but I didn't even have the energy to start the paperwork to submit a complaint to the warden. I just wanted to do my time and go home.

I was past being upset at Glo. I just wanted to solidify a working arrangement to see my baby girl and keep tabs and a tight grip on her while I was inside. It was important that Nia understood the importance of respecting her mother regardless of her choices.

That was how I was raised and that was how I was raising Nia. It didn't help that Glo was creating an environment that would force Nia to have to choose who she had to listen to.

Had Gloria been arrested, and I was her son's guardian, I would've upheld the rules she implemented. When you let kids think they didn't have to listen to other adults, it created a power dynamic and increased conflict. You can't create that kind of divide in front of children. Glo and I were supposed to be tag teaming Nia. We were supposed to be on the same page — especially when it came to laying down the law. It seemed like Glo and Nia had teamed up against me."

CHAPTER 23

HARMONY

the quality of forming a pleasing and consistent whole.

Unfortunately, as Ora kept talking, my level of peace slowly faded away. She was so broken, and it was impossible to drown her out. Her energy was immensely penetrating. The Bible says, "bad company corrupts good character," and the more I stayed in that cell with her, the higher the emotional rollercoasters would be. She'd take me up with her humming, singing, and dancing. She would read out of the Bible, murmuring and rolling the scriptures over and over until she was ready to shout them out loud.

"Thank you, Jesus. Thank you, Father! MY REDEEMER! MY HEALER! OH JESUS. BEHOLD JESUS. FORGIVE ME FOR I HAVE SINNED," she would scream.

After the second day she did this, I realized I couldn't beat her, so I had to join her. I used this time to pray and worship God with her. I would call out some scriptures, and she would join in with me. Once I settled in with the fact that this would be my daily routine until I left, I got into it. We'd pray and shout and worship for forty-five minutes 'til an hour. I always felt relieved and full of the Holy Spirit.

I thanked God that despite my parents' addiction, I was raised in the church. I had my Daddy and his mom to thank for that. My father's mother kept us in Sunday school weekly and choir practice twice a week. Gloria and I were both raised in the church. I'm not sure about Glo, but I always knew how to tap into my spirituality.

My faith in God kept me going throughout the years. I knew all I had to do was repent for forgiveness and pray for guidance. Once I sealed my prayer with, "Amen, in the name of Jesus," it was activated. My daddy taught me this as a child, and it stuck with me. My infamous prayer before I would go into Macy's on Thirty-Fourth Street to steal was, "Father God, forgive me for the crimes I am about to commit. Continue to guide me down a path of righteousness as I navigate this life. In Jesus name, Amen."

It was that prayer that saved me many times from getting arrested. Anytime I said that prayer, I never got caught. I usually got caught when I was with someone or a group of other boosters who were anxious and jittery. Their nervousness threw me off my game, and I'd forget to say my prayer, and before I knew it, I was swept up by loss prevention.

After getting busted about my third time, I started making my store runs alone. I would hire a driver, who was actually one of my regular customers in Brevoort at the time, and she would take me to the various malls and shopping centers. Whenever I rode alone with no tag alongs, I was in and out like a robbery. Literally. I didn't have to worry about anyone blowing my cover or looking at me for too long when I rolled solo. I didn't have to worry about guiding any bag up girls and making sure they bagged up the clothes neatly and as flat as possible.

I wore a girdle and a jean skirt that I could hide mink coats under. Any good thief knew how to steal furs. As Jay-Z said, "there's no reward without risk" and coming up on a mink, sherling, or persian lamb was some sweet cash, tax free. You could easily make $1200-$1500 at an instant if you had a stylish fur and working customers.

Despite my criminal mind and stinkin' thinking, I always believed in God, and I always knew that God loved me, which was why he protected me from all the traps I set myself, and for that I was grateful. The one thing I so desperately prayed for during that particular session with Ora was to restore my relationship with Gloria and Nia. I also prayed for Nia's protection from the streets and her own fleshly desires.

As I hummed to myself with my head down and my eyes closed, I smelled Ora get near. She grabbed my hand and held it in hers. She started singing out loud. Her voice was raspy and powerful, and this was the first time I heard her belt out a song loudly. She usually just hummed. She opened her mouth and sang:

If tomorrow is judgment day
And I'm standing on the front line
And the Lord asks me what I did with my life
I will say I spent it with you
'Cause your love is my love And my love is your love
It would take an eternity to break us
And the chains of Amistad couldn't hold us

I JOINED in with her on the famous Whitney Houston tune, and I was pretty sure we woke up many napping inmates. Although I wasn't one to draw attention to my cell, my heart was so moved by the Spirit and the harmony of our voices as we sang the music. We finished the song, and I was exhausted. I grabbed a bottle of water from near my bed, and tore the cap off. I was so out of breath from singing that I guzzled down the entire bottle without pausing even a second to breathe. Never underestimate the power of water in a feat of tired desperation.

The more I observed Ora, the more curious I became. She had no problem questioning me, so why did I have an issue with getting into her business?

"Ora?"

"Yaa gal," she answered.

"You said you're here for your husband's death, right?"

She stayed quiet, which came by surprise because she always had a remark or rebuttal.

"No suh. De judge say so. Mi nuh know how he die. But whet mi doh know is he ass dead. Mi af no reason fuh tell story, gal. Wheteva happen to he — he deserve it. De mon abuse me fuh years. In fact, de mon does more than abuse mi gal, de mon took away mi hope. Mi tink mi af a godfearing mon, but mi af a flesh fearing mon. Oyyy Selassie this, Selassie that. Selassie never save nobody! Tey only one Savior, and he name Jesus Christ, mon. De mon woh driving me crazy, gal. Between he tryn manage mi hole life, de fights that led to miscarriage after miscarriage 'til mi can't conceive no more. Mi waste a lot of time wid he."

I was a little confused. For the most part, I understood what she said, but I wondered who Selassie was. I didn't want to look ignorant, so I just shook my head disappointedly.

Ora seemed to pick up on my ignorance and said,

"Mi husband he a Rasta Mon. Mi was ah Rasta too. We rastas honor Selassie. Haile Selassie. At first, mi tink di lifestyle not too bad, natural and low maintenance. Mi ah neva know how much sadness it would bring me."

Determined to cheer her up and perhaps get a smile, I asked her,

"If you could do one thing different to change your life, what would you do?"

"Mi would choose a different mon. Mi would choose a better mon."

CHAPTER 24

SURPRISE

an unexpected or astonishing event, fact, or thing.

Ora wasn't too bad. I learned early on that everyone in jail had a story, and most people just needed someone to listen to them. We all needed people to listen to us without the need to respond but to understand us. The truth of the matter was, I had hope. I had my entire life to look forward to. Ora didn't. She spent most of her life with a man who ruled over her, and she was now sixty-four years old with nothing or anyone to look forward to but the joy of the Lord.

Knowing this made me more compassionate towards her. My tolerance for her instantly increased. As soon as my tolerance grew, her smell began to fade. The more you grow to like or love someone, the more tolerance you grow for them. I had to make it comfortable while I was here, so getting on good terms with Ora was the best thing I could have done.

This newly found peace filled our cell. It allowed Ora and I to co-exist in love and without strife. I just didn't have the energy to be in strife. I was looking towards the future. I had a lot to be thankful for. My commissary was loaded with cash. I had less than 180 days to serve, and for the most part, I knew my daughter was safe and sound. In all actuality, I had little to worry about.

Reconciling with Ora gave me the desire to want to reconcile with Glo. The truth of the matter was, I needed her. I needed us to get along for the sake of Nia and my mental health. Now was not the time to be beefing with my sister while she assumed guardianship over my daughter. Pam was right. I had to do whatever — kiss ass or play phony to get what I needed. Maintaining a relationship with Nia while I served the rest of my sentence was my number one priority. I was determined to apologize and show deference to Glo if that meant being involved in Nia's life.

I was determined to call and make up with Glo. I made it up in my mind that the first thing I would say on the phone was sorry. I couldn't afford for this conversation to go left. After lunch, all of the inmates lined up outside the phone booth area to make calls. I stood in the line feeling excited and lighthearted. When I got to the front of the line and dialed Glo's cell phone number, it didn't even ring; it went straight to voicemail. I called back twice, and it went to voicemail every time.

I finally decided to call Tony. I gave him a day to cool off. I just wanted everything to go back to how it was. I was just ready to start anew with everyone. I punched his number into the phone, and it rang two times until someone answered the phone. I could hear breathing that sounded muffled on the other end. I was so excited that he answered.

"Tony. Baby. It's Joi. Can you hear me?"

I continued to hear breathing on the other end. The breath got progressively louder. Confused, I repeated myself.

"Tony, it's Joi. Can you hear me, baby?"

"Yuh messing wid a married mon and dun kno him real name. It Rodnell. Don't call dis hea phone again, bitch."

Click.

The phone went blank, and instantaneously my body got chills.

That couldn't have been anyone but his wife, who was dead wrong. Tony told me his first name was Rodnell, but I preferred to call him Tony. I could tell she was worried about the wrong thing anyway. Instead of worrying about the name I call your husband, how about you worry about him using his hard-earned money to replenish my commissary or coming to visit me and looking after Nia momentarily. In the words of Kanye West, "you worried 'bout the wrong thing, the wrong thing." All I could do was laugh.

I walked back towards my cell with a smirk on my face. If his wife, who he clearly didn't want to be with, wanted action, I'd give it to her. Some bitches just didn't get it. That man showed her at the market in Jamaica he didn't want her when he tore her hands off of him and walked off with me. I'm pretty sure she saw me from afar as we walked away together. Like Tony said, if it wasn't me, it was going to be someone other than his wife. That had nothing to do with me. Tony already made up his mind.

I guess I could imagine how it would feel to know that your husband wasn't only cheating, but he was cheating because he didn't want you. Cheating occurred for many reasons, which in most cases, wasn't because the man wasn't happy with his woman. We could blame sexism, patriarchy, and misogyny — among many others — as to why men cheated. In my opinion, if your man was cheating on you because he was unhappy and didn't want you, you should absolutely and expeditiously leave that relationship. I would. But she'll learn sooner or later.

Before I could make my way back to my cell, I was stopped by a female guard. She was Spanish and all of 4'11". She looked me up and down before saying, "Holloway. We've been looking for you for a few minutes. You have a visitor in the waiting area."

Tony was here to surprise me again, I thought. But then again, I just called his phone, and his wife answered. He wouldn't travel without his phone, so it couldn't have been him. I was anxious to know who it was. I nodded in agreement with the guard and proceeded to turn around for her to handcuff me and escort me to the visiting area. Today was such a good day, it looked brighter in the jail and not the usual somber ambience. As soon as I stepped into the visiting area, still handcuffed, I spotted Gloria and Nia sitting in two plastic chairs.

My heart instantly lit up with joy. I couldn't believe they were here. They were the last people I expected to see. I was convinced it was Tony coming back to apologize and tell me he missed me. This was a way better surprise. One thing I was sure of was that God answered prayers. I asked him to help restore my relationship with my sister and daughter and before twenty-four hours passed, they appeared. The Holy Spirit interceded many times during prayer, directing God to bring what's near to you. When tapped in with the Holy Spirit, you can hear God speak to you and direct you on what to pray for, manifesting and bringing it close to you. God heard my prayer and answered it.

The guard uncuffed me, and I scurried over to the plastic chairs in Glo's direction first. I was so grateful that she brought Nia to see me. It showed me that she had a heart and still loved me, and despite any sister rivalry, she had the heart to do what was right. A tear came down my cheek. Glo stood up from her chair, and I threw my arms around her excitedly to greet me. She had a soft grin plastered across her face that turned into an ear-to-ear smile when I hugged her.

"Thank you so much, Glo, for coming and bringing Nia. I appreciate you so much, and I am so sorry..."

"Nah, sister. I'm sorry for the way I was acting. I just wanted to keep Nia safe and protect her while you were away. Things just went left when Tony went to pick her up from school. I was worried about my niece."

"I know and I'm sorry. That wasn't cool. I was just still so upset about you not answering the phone the day Pam fell, so I didn't call you."

"Joi. It's been stressful dealing with Pam, but I'm sorry about that too," Glo said before she took a seat.

I glanced over at Nia, who was dressed in a school uniform — a yellow shirt, navy-blue khaki pants, and blue dress shoes. Her hair was braided in a juvenile-like style. The braids didn't do much for her gorgeous face, but that was the least of my concerns. At least Glo was dressing her appropriately.

"Stand up, baby girl, give me a hug."

Nia got up quickly and wrapped her arms around my waist tightly. I soaked in the embrace, which felt so good. Nothing beat the feeling of a child missing you. This is exactly what I needed.

I sat down with solace in my heart and looked straight ahead at Nia. Nothing but joy filled my heart at the moment. Glo sat back in her chair with a confused grin on her face.

"You good, Glo? How was the ride here?" I asked.

Glo looked a bit startled. She wiped her eyes and took a deep breath.

"Yeah, it was cool, sister. I'm just a little tired," she said before taking a big yawn. She reached out her arms to stretch then sat up straight in the seat.

"What about you, sister? How you managing in here?"

"Same ole shit. Just a different day. I'm holding my head, just praying this time goes as fast as it came."

CHAPTER 25

FORGIVENESS

the act of forgiveness, to cease to feel resentment against

Not only did Gloria surprise me, but her actions were surprisingly and favorably unpredictable as well. I had no idea that she planned to come see me, but I was relieved. We didn't need to be at odds with one another. It definitely didn't make me feel any better. Knowing that I could rely on my sister made me feel confident and comfortable.

Every inmate wanted to know they had at least one person in their corner on the outside. With Pam in the nursing home and not easily accessible, Gloria was my trusted go to. Knowing that there was no beef or strife between us made it easier to sleep.

Overall, my first week in prison turned out to be okay. I experienced a few bumps in the road, but I was blessed to have a commissary full of money and three visits in a week. Not everyone in prison could relate. As much as I didn't want visitors, it still felt good to know I had people who cared enough to visit me. When you're not a big shot, a killer, or drug lord, anything anybody does for you while you're in prison is love. Because they absolutely owe you nothing. I woke up the next day with a joyous heart.

Ora had slept the entire night without any outbursts, and I was grateful. She woke up with another song on her heart, and we sang and prayed. I stretched my limbs and belted out my morning yawns. Forgiveness really lightens your spirit. You feel free once you forgive and let go. To be frank, I didn't have the time and I couldn't afford to still be angry at Glo. It was time to think forward and move on. I so desperately wanted to start over as soon as I was released.

My main goal was to keep the peace with Glo while incarcerated so that talking with Nia would go smoothly. All in all, we were grateful to have Pam as a mom. She did instill a basic level of loyalty in both of us, to have the best interest of each other when it came down to difficult and uncomfortable situations. We knew not to turn on each other or each other's kids. We may have done small things to spite each other, but Glo coming to visit me showed that she still had love for me.

Even talking with her regarding the order of protection against Tony made me understand how much she loved me and Nia. Her genuine concern became clearer after we talked.

Glo just wanted to make sure that Nia was okay. I could understand her concern for not trusting Tony, especially considering the last incident with Clyde as well as the fact that she didn't know Tony well enough. I wasn't stubborn enough to dismiss the validity in that. I will admit that I was super upset about Glo allowing Nia to stay out 'til 11pm, and I simply wanted to take the reins again. I was determined to go to war with Glo just to ensure that Nia was properly supervised and guided.

To be truthful, I was so fueled with anger towards Glo that I wanted to leave her out of it and get to Nia first and foremost, even if that meant putting her in harm's way. And that's where I was wrong. Anger cannot consume you to the point to where you make risky decisions just to seek revenge or wrath on another. I was happy that I was mature enough to recognize that my anger was a problem. Not that I didn't have a right to be angry, but essentially, no one had the right to be angry for anger does not produce the righteousness of God.

Anger is an emotion that God speaks against in the Bible. My sessions with Ora had revealed that to me. In Ephesians, he says, "Get rid of all bitterness, rage, anger, harsh words, and slander, as well as all types of evil behavior. Instead, be kind to each other, tender-hearted, forgiving one another, just as God through Christ has forgiven you."

I had to admit that God forgave me time and time again for shoplifting, for judging others, and overwhelming them with negative speech. So, it was my turn to forgive Gloria, regardless of anything she had done. The more I stayed angry, the more my heart hardened, and I refused to be bitter.

Perspective is so important when faced with trials and tribulations. How you look at the situation you're faced with makes a complete difference in how you handle it. I could've chosen to be upset at Glo, upset at the judge, or even upset at Tony, but the truth of the matter was that I had to accept the role I played in all of this. I had to accept that the decisions I made years ago were presently affecting me, and that was nobody's fault but mine. With maturity came accountability and responsibility.

I was proud that at thirty-one, I could recognize the mistakes I'd made and had the courage to correct them. First, with correcting my mentality, the hardest thing to break. I knew that I had to change my mindset if I wanted to do things differently once released. And I was prepared to face my demons and make better choices.

Ora had a lot to do with this. Although Ora had been through a lot, she wasn't bitter. She made peace with the life she chose, and she faced her demons head on, and even shared them with me. Her vulnerability was so inspiring and moving, it made me realize that I had the power to change, forgive, and move on.

I was happy that it only took a week for me to take on this new attitude. I was thankful Glo and I had reconciled, and I was happy to know that she was taking the Auntie role seriously because I desperately needed her. We all needed her. Me, Pam, Nia, and her son. I had to accept that although I was the older and wiser one, I was of no help at the present moment. I couldn't do anything, so essentially; I really couldn't say anything.

Yes, I was mad that Gloria had me removed as Pam's legal proxy and even lied to Pam about my approval, but ultimately, I didn't have the liberty to make fast, effective decisions regarding her health. Not being present at the nursing home, not being able to visit Pam or make my presence known amongst the nursing staff or speak with her doctors, really impacted my knowledge about what was going on as well as my ability to speak on Pam's behalf. The best thing was for Gloria to take over. Well, for now. It was very important that Glo and I were on good terms so I could guide and advise her, and we could make decisions as a unit.

Truth be told, I was proud of Glo. She was holding it all down. She was holding us all down. She had her shit with her like we all do, but she rose to the occasion and executed when we needed her. She was willing to make tough decisions to serve the greater good of the situation at hand. As soon as I got locked up, the pressing matter at hand was Nia's supervision and wellbeing. I had to act fast, and I chose to call Tony. He delivered Nia safely to Glo's, which I was grateful for. Please understand that I did not call Tony to spite my sister. I called Tony because I knew he would answer the phone, and I wasn't too sure if Glo would.

Glo's unreliability regarding Pam when she fell traumatized me. She didn't answer the phone all night while I was in the hospital with Pam, and I just couldn't risk her not answering. I was mad at her for a while — until I stopped and realized how much she had on her plate. Understanding can help aid in forgiveness as well.

As much as I disliked my sister at times, I was grateful I had one. If I didn't have Glo, I would have been shit out of luck many times if I had to solely rely on Pam. Sisters were supposed to love and protect like no other. That didn't mean they liked you all the time. That didn't mean you are girlfriends and have everything in common. It didn't mean you agreed on everything, or that you shared all of the same morals or principles.

Glo and I differed in a lot of our thoughts, beliefs, and patterns, but we shared the same principle of love, loyalty, and protectiveness over each other. We might've cursed each other out and fought, but we always came together when it mattered. We always showed up for each other whenever we needed to. And that I was thankful for despite it all.

* * *

"HEY, baby. How you doing? How's school?"

"School's okay," she whispered. Nia sounded a bit down on the phone when I spoke to her the next day.

"How're your classes going?" I continued to pry.

Nia remained quiet for nearly two minutes. I resisted the urge to badger her any further. Just when I decided to give up, she spoke.

"My classes are fine, Ma. But I want to go home. Sleep in my bed. I'm tired of sleeping on the couch at Auntie's house. I can't wait for you to come home."

"Aww, baby. I can't wait to come home either. Don't you worry, I'll be home soon. Love you. Now put your Auntie on the phone."

Glo maintained the same chipper energy she had displayed when she visited. It was nice to talk to her without any hostility, bad vibes, or weird energy. It felt good to have my sister back. Periodically throughout the years, we would go through a period of maybe four to five months where things were cordial, and we spoke more, and even hung out sometimes. But it never lasted the whole year. Normally, as the holidays neared, we'd be at each other's throats again, and we'd force smiles and hugs on Thanksgiving and Christmas to please Pam.

Pam was the trunk to our family tree. She held us all up and together. Without the trunk, the tree couldn't stand, and branches wouldn't even grow. Gloria and I were the branches. Likewise, without Pam, we couldn't exist. I was thankful that Pam's presence forced us to always reconcile. Usually, Pam's advice was always for me to be the bigger person.

"Why me, ma? Why I always have to be the bigger person when she's always wrong?"

Pam would grab my teenage face, cupping my chin with two thumbs and say, "Because you're the oldest, the smartest, and the strongest, and that's what comes with the role. You can't choose it. It's given to you, sweetheart."

She would kiss my forehead and rub it in with her right thumb. As I got older, she continued to tell me the same thing in different renditions. My favorite one was on the phone when she would end it with, "Ciao."

She'd say, "Sista Suki, you know you're older and smarter. Be the bigger person always. That's how you get ya blessings. Talk to you later, baby. Ciao."

She would hang up, and I'd always laugh. I would call her back a few days later and tell her either I apologized to Glo or made up with her and she'd always say, "That's a beautiful thing."

I sure missed that lady. I was grateful that Glo and me were getting along so great that I didn't even bother asking her about Pam. Now that I knew I could talk to Pam myself, I decided that I would get the information directly from the source. If I had any concerns, then I would approach Glo. I'm sure if there was anything pressing regarding Pam's health, Gloria would be forthcoming with the information. I just didn't want to spark any drama or argument with Glo when we were just getting back on good terms.

I returned to my cell to find Ora writing in a notebook while she sat with headphones in her ears. She noticed me as I walked in and looked up and smiled in my direction. She continued to hum to herself for the next five minutes. Abruptly, she stopped humming and took off her headset and threw it down.

"Gal, when last yuh talk tuh yuh mudda?"

Was this woman reading my mind? I was missing Pam and planning to place my very next phone call to the nursing home.

"About three or four days ago. She's doing good. I'm gonna call her later tonight."

"Mhmm. Yea call she. Mi feel she miss yuh," she responded.

"Yeah, I miss her too. Things are going so much better with my sister and my daughter. I'm able to talk to Nia everyday now. My sister agreed to bring her to see me twice a week. My sister has really adjusted her attitude, and I'm adjusting mine. She's holding down everything now, and I'm so proud of her and grateful for her."

"Tat gud, gyal. Hold mi hand. Mi feel we should pray fuh yuh mudda and yuh sister."

I didn't oppose. I knew not to. Ora was a bit extreme, but she meant well. Her spirituality rubbed off on me. I got used to praying two to three times a day with her. It was helpful in maintaining my peace while on the inside. Ora got up from her bed and grabbed both of my hands.

"Heavenly Fadda, thank yuh fuh this holy day. Wea two come fawad humbly asking fuh peace and harmony in we soul. We receive de Holy Spirit fuh carry we true we sentences and beyond. Fada please bless tis woman Joi and she family – bless she mudda, bless she fadda and she rasshole sista. Equip Joi wid de spirit of forgiveness, casting dung de spirit of rage an bitterness despite any occurrences. Fadda God mi declare no weapon shall form against she. In Jesus Name, we say Amen.

My heart instantly felt lighter.

"In Jesus name, I receive that. Thank you, Ora, for your prayerful blessings."

Ora smiled at me, and I smiled back. I never felt this good in jail before.

* * *

SURPRISINGLY, dinner didn't look too bad tonight. The chicken looked decently cooked, and the mashed potatoes didn't taste too bad. I took a forkful of the mashed potatoes and was surprised that I was able to swallow it. Just thankful for a digestible meal, I ditched the soggy green vegetables though. Truthfully, I was looking forward to my salmon and rice I got from the commissary. I didn't really trust the correctional facility to feed inmates quality food. I would've rather bought mine because even though it was more expensive than the supermarket prices, I was able to prepare it, and I knew what went into it. Either way, my spirits were high and nothing about now could bring me down.

After dinner, I parted ways with Ora while she headed back to the cell, and I made my way to the phone booth area with the rest of the ladies to make our last evening calls. We all lined up, waiting for the guard to open the door and allow us in the big phone booth room.

When it was my turn, I dialed the nursing home telephone number, and a busy signal instantly played. Then, I remembered that I punched the last two numbers in wrong, so I hung up and punched in each number carefully. The phone started to ring. One. Two. Three rings, no answer. On the fourth ring, someone finally answered.

"Hello, thanks for calling the Cobble Hill Patient Facility. This is the nursing's station; how may I direct your call?"

"Hi. My name is Joi-Ann Holloway. I am calling to speak with my mother, Pamela Holloway. Is she available to talk?"

The other line went dead, so I said, "Hello?"

"Hold please, ma'am," the voice said back quickly and emotionless.

"Okay," I softly replied.

The voice on the other end sounded like a young Hispanic woman — someone I never spoke with before, so I wasn't sure if she even knew Pam, which was almost impossible. Pam's bubbly personality and feisty comebacks were hard for anyone to forget. She lit up the room with her infectious smile and nostalgic slang words.

Her vocabulary always made you laugh because she would use complex words in such a casual, ebonic way. Her favorite word for me and Gloria was uncouth. Whenever we were suspended from school or detained for fighting, Mommy would always say, "You're so uncouth. You girls have no tact, damn it."

I'm sure Pam had the nursing staff cracking up at her jokes because she always made me laugh — even when she was cursing me out. After what seemed like an eternity, someone finally came to the phone and answered it.

"Hello, Ms. Holloway. How are you doing today?"

"I'm doing good today. I'm in great spirits. Just looking to check in on my mom. Is she available to talk? If not, I'll just call back tomorrow. I know she has rehab and dialysis that keeps her busy."

I HEARD silence again after I finished my sentence.

"Hello. Are you there? Can I speak with my mother, Pamela Holloway?"

It seemed like there were some connection issues with the phone because I had to keep repeating myself.

"Ms. Holloway, I regret to inform you that your mother, Pamela, passed away three days ago from a severe case of cirrhosis, liver failure with gastrointestinal bleeding. When the nurses checked on her in the morning, her skin and eyes were stark yellow. Your sister, Gloria, signed off on the body two days ago. The body was transported to a funeral home in Brooklyn this morning. I am so sorry to break the news to you. My condolences go out to you and your family. Please be well."

I heard a click, and I dropped the phone. Tears fell from my eyes, and my body dropped to the floor.

CHAPTER 26

BITTERSWEET

both bitter and sweet to the taste, both pleasant and painful or regretful:

29 Hours Later

My body rocked back and forth uncontrollably, hitting the hard-pressed leather seat on the transport bus that transported me back to court. It was past the crack of dawn. The sun was out, and the birds were chirping. Contrary to the visual, I had no zeal or life left in me. I only had rage.

My best friend, my only confidant was gone.

I didn't even get to say goodbye. I didn't even get to say I love you one last time.

By the time the bus reached One Centre Street in Manhattan, the sun disappeared, and a gloomy overcast masked the sky, turning what seemed to look like a chipper day into a shadowy, somber, sunken place.

Aggressively, the guard pulled me up from my seat and escorted me by the arm into the court building. I held my head down, not in embarrassment but utter defeat.

How could I go on? I had no one.

My feet dragged on the floor as the guard struggled to carry my weight as he walked me into the building. Once inside the courtroom, after the intensive anal body search, I was met by my lawyer, who looked just as lachrymose as me sitting dreadfully on the bench.

She stood as soon as she saw me.

"May I, Officer?" She directed her question to the guard before hugging me.

"I'm terribly sorry, Joi. I am going to request two weeks for funeral preparation, actual service, and pain and suffering. I wish I could push to drop all charges, but the case has been adjourned, and only the judge has the authority. Let's hope for the best," she pleaded and squeezed my hand after unlocking from my embrace.

I was at a loss for words. I didn't even look at her. The guard followed me as I took my seat on the crowded bench in the first row, where my lawyer's briefcase sat. It was crowded in here. I could tell it was going to be a long wait from the mixture of body odors, perfume, and cologne, masking the aroma and making the space claustrophobic. I still had not looked up. At this point, I was slouching terribly with a very uncomfortable looking hunchback.

After unconsciously napping for what seemed like forever, I heard my name called. Standing in front of the same dickhead judge who sent me to jail when I was just tryna do the right thing by my moms and still obey that bullshit court order, burned me like hell.

My lawyer said to me quietly, "Don't worry, Joi. I'm hopeful."

Before my lawyer could get to speak her piece, the judge said,

"Rest, Counselor. May I have a moment?"

"Your honor," my lawyer nodded her head forward.

"Many times, in this field, you see repeat offenders concoct stories and fabricate illnesses to get out of court mandated programs. In my thirty years of doing this, I can attest that I have seen it all. Therefore, I take these kinds of cases seriously. However, Ms. Holloway, on behalf of myself and the court, we openly express our deepest condolences for your loss. With much talk to the prosecutor's office, we have moved to dismiss your case and drop all charges. This court hereby grants the dismissal of all charges for Joyce-Ann Holloway. You are free to go. Counselor, thank you for your time." My lawyer jumped from her seat expeditiously.

"Thank you, your honor," she responded.

"Bailiff, please remove these handcuffs." The bailiff walked over to me quickly in response to my lawyer's demand.

As soon as the shackles were released, I raised my hands in bittersweet victory, simultaneously praising and thanking God for my freedom, yet afraid it'd soon be stripped away again.

THE BRASH, biting and bitter wind stung my face more than anywhere else on my body as I stood, shivering outside City Hall, directly across from Brooklyn Bridge. It was awfully cold for October —especially on the outside. Rikers wasn't nearly as cold. In a matter of a week, the weather had gotten colder, shocking my body because I had spent most of last week indoors.

Tony picked up my clothes when I first got booked, so I walked out of there with nothing, just the clothes on my back — a long, black shirt with some gray slacks and dress shoes. No coat, jacket, or sweater. Luckily, my lawyer let me use her cell to make a few calls, all to which were to no avail. Glo didn't answer after I tried both the house phone and her cell. Neither did Tony. I also shot them both a text. My lawyer was even nice enough to treat me to a cup of tea and a cheese Danish as she gracefully and patiently allowed thirty minutes for a call back. Neither Glo nor Tony returned my call.

With not even two dollars to hop on the A train, I took a deep breath and crossed the street to the bridge intersection and began trudging my way over the Brooklyn Bridge.

I continued to look straight ahead, fighting the urge to look down at the broken wood pieces that protruded under my feet. I always hated walking the Brooklyn Bridge. I preferred The Williamsburg Bridge, which was much more reliable as it was sturdy and solid. The clouds gloomed in the air with a dull overcast, signaling that rain would soon come.

I dug my hands in my pockets and quickened my steps. I was determined to beat the rain.

Three hours later, I made it to the front of Glo's apartment. It took me about two hours; I'm assuming to walk over the bridge. Winded, tired, and out of breath, I hopped the turnstile at Jay Street and boarded the local 8th Avenue line. I noticed on the huge clock in the train station that it was three pm when I boarded the train.

I rubbed my hands together and took a deep breath before knocking on the door. After three loud gongs, the gold peephole flashed open.

"Auntie. It's my mother." Nia's voice was low and flat.

Thirty seconds later, the door opened, where Nia stood tall and unimpressed with her elbows folded and her hips pushed out to the side.

"Mommy, what you doing here? I didn't know you were coming home today."

"Neither did I. The court dropped the charges once they found out your grandma died."

Nia still hadn't let me inside.

"Baby, move aside and let me in."

She hesitated then backed up into the house.

"Where's Gloria?" I asked.

"How did you find out Grandma died?" she asked inquisitively.

As soon as I turned the corner, I saw Gloria crouched down on the living room floor covered with documents that looked like mail, bills, and other important paperwork.

"Nia, go in the back with your cousin," I said, turning to Nia. "But Mommy, how did you find out Grandma died?"

"NIA. STOP QUESTIONING ME AND TAKE YOUR ASS IN YOUR COUSIN'S ROOM NOW!"

Nia unfolded her elbows and put them on her hips defiantly. She rolled her eyes and looked me boldly in the eye.

"Auntie, do you still need my help?"

Gloria looked up quickly, completely ignoring me and my entire presence.

"Not right now, Mamacita. Do what your mother says."

"Okay," she muttered disappointedly before she turned her back to me and rushed to the room.

What the fuck has gotten into Nia? This little bitch was testing my patience bad. She thinks because I was in jail for a week that I won't kindly go back for beating her ass? Ain't no child of mine disrespecting me. First Nia, now I gotta address this witch, Gloria.

"Glo. So, you thought I wasn't gon' find out that Pam died? You think because I was locked up that I wasn't checking on Pam? Just when the fuck were you gonna tell me that our mother died?"

Sitting on the floor with her knees to her chin, Gloria looked up with tears in her eyes.

"I just couldn't tell you while you were in jail. I'm so sorry."

"Bullshit, Gloria. Bullshit. You didn't plan on telling me. I'm so sick of your shit. You put my mother in a nursing home and you let her die!" I screamed irately.

Emotionally enraged yet emotionless, I kicked her in the face so hard she fell back on the floor. I jumped on top of her and began wailing uncontrollably with my fists. Before I knew it, I held her neck comfortably in between my two hands as I yelled "I hate you" over and over.

To my surprise, I suddenly felt a wrenching pain in my back. It wasn't until the third strike that I noticed Nia hitting me with a heavy, steel dustpan.

"Get the fuck off of my aunt and get the fuck out!" she screamed.

Neglecting Glo, who was now free of my wrath, I jumped up so quickly, ready to get a piece of Nia.

I charged ahead at Nia and yanked the long dustpan handle from her.

"YOU LITTLE BITCH! You gonna turn on your own mother?"

I grabbed her towards me and smacked her so hard, I left a slight print on her light-skinned face. Before I could push her on the couch, I collapsed to the ground and began to see black. All I remember hearing were flying curse words from both Gloria and Nia, but I couldn't make out what they were saying. Once I rolled over, I saw my daughter kicking me while Gloria spat on me over and over. Helplessly unable to move, my body began to shiver from the excess saliva on my face.

CHAPTER 27

JAIL BIRD

a person who is or has been in prison, especially a criminal who has been jailed repeatedly, a habitual criminal.

In jail, I felt alone. But out here with Pam gone and my daughter and my sister tag teaming me, I truly was alone. After our fight, I woke up in Gloria's apartment, laying on the couch with a blanket over me. Although shirtless, I noticed I still had a bra on from the uncomfortable underwire that pierced me under the breast.

Once awake, I got up and roamed the apartment. It was pitch black outside, except for the dimly lit street posts that slightly illuminated the project walkways. Unaware of the time, I peeked inside Gloria's room, where she was spread out wildly asleep on her bed. I rushed back to the living room and picked up the house phone and dialed Tony.

He answered on the second ring.

"Tony. It's Joi. I was released. I need my car and house keys. Please come pick me up from my sister's."

Although Tony basically dumped me while I was locked up, he kept his word and showed up like he said he would when I was released. Without hesitation, he was there within twenty minutes.

I tried to wake Nia from sleep, begging her to come home with me. She fought hard not to, so I left.

Fuck it. I could use my first night back home kid free.

* * *

"GLORIA, how you expect not only me but my man to be chauffeuring you all around to handle this shit with no money in our pockets? You got back fifty thousand dollars from Pam's insurance, and I can't get a thousand dollars? You know I lost my job and just came home. What the fuck?!"

I couldn't believe that Pam signed over my legal rights as her beneficiary and proxy to Glo. I couldn't believe Pam died so quickly before I could get released and be made her proxy again. I wasn't sweating it, though, because most of that money was going to Pam's funeral arrangements, her burial, and plot. She had money designated for her headstone, as well as a tree she requested to be planted, along with a stone bench placed next to the headstone for her visitors to sit by her. I was almost certain that Gloria would do right by Pam and honor what she left in her will.

I was shocked that Pam even had a will so soon. She hadn't even reached sixty years old. Yet, knowing my boujee ass grandmother, I shouldn't have been surprised at all. She was planning Pam's death from the time she was born. Pam started shooting dope as early as Nia started having sex, and my grandmother just turned her head. So enthralled in her Eastern Star sisters and obsessed with her best friend's grandchildren, who were college educated and graduated, married with homes, and two parent households, that she neglected her own family.

She was proud of her best friend's family because they did things the right way. They gave her something to be proud of. They reaffirmed her belief in the American Dream rhetoric. We didn't. We were ghetto, lazy, and troubled — what my grandmother considered blasphemy. West Indians didn't come to the land of opportunity and get hooked on drugs. They might as well have stayed in their third world country. Although my grandmother loved my mother very much, she couldn't understand why and how her daughter allowed drugs to take over her life.

"Joi-Ann, I can't give you more than gas money. This money has to cover the funeral."

"Gloria, you know damn well you could spare me a thousand dollars. That's all I'm asking for. I need it right now. I got a car note and insurance coming up with no job."

"Well, I ain't never have no job, and you don't see me complaining. That's why I don't got no car yet. I stay in my lane."

"You don't got no job 'cause you don't want no job. You could have a car if you wanted one."

"Yeah, and trust I'll be getting one soon. Thanks to Pam. So, nah, I can't give you no thousand dollars, Joyce," she said.

"Well, I need something more than thirty dollars for gas, so what are we doing? I need like three hundred dollars."

"Joi, don't be stupid with the demands 'cause I only got seventy-five dollars for you, and you better make do. I mean, I could call a cab and you just meet me down there. Yeah, how about we do that? I'm good. I'll see you down there. The address is 467 Pacific Street on the corner of Classon Avenue. Now I can just use that seventy-five dollars for my cab there, back, and lunch."

THE FUNERAL PARLOR reeked of beautifully arranged death with a touch of celebration. I sat in the funeral director's office in an uncomfortable, leather chair next to Gloria. It had been forty-five minutes, and Gloria had made all of the decisions without asking for my opinion.

"Have you ladies decided on a color for the casket?"

"What are our options?" I asked.

"Didn't your sister show you the pamphlet with the various color options?" he asked inquisitively.

Before I could answer no, Gloria dug into her bag and pulled out an eight by eleven tri-fold brochure. She opened it and planted it on the desk, separating us from the funeral director.

"Mr. Mercer, I absolutely love the sage color. Can we get that one? Gloria held her index finger down on the center of the brochure, highlighting the soft green.

"Is there a Lavender option? That was Mommy's favorite color."

"Actually, there is. Let me show ..."

Abruptly and hastily, Gloria interjected.

"Mr. Mercer, we're certain. I'm certain about the sage option."

Fed up and disgusted, I held my head down in my hands, just waiting for this shit to end. Unexpectedly, I felt my cell phone begin to vibrate in my purse. I pulled it out and looked at the caller ID. It read, "Bedford Hills Correctional Facility." Curious, I answered the phone quickly.

"Excuse me, sir. I have to take this call," I said to the funeral director.

Before I could get up to step out and take my call, I heard an operator say, "You have a call from an inmate at Bedford Hills Correctional Facility." Within seconds, I heard a familiar voice on the other end.

"Joi. Is this Joi Holloway? It's Bobby."

Surprised, I fanned my hand in silence.

"Hi, Bobby. Yes, it's me, Joi."

"Hold on, sir. My mother's husband is on the phone. May he hear what's going on?" I asked the funeral director.

Full of indifference, the funeral director shrugged his shoulders.

"I guess. I don't see why not," he said.

I put the call on speaker and said, "Bobby, can you hear us?"

"Yes, yes. I can hear you."

"Gloria and I are here with the funeral director, looking at the color options for the casket and some other things."

"Okay, that sounds good, Joi. Tell Gloria I said hi."

"She's right here. She can hear you."

Glo screwed up her face and rolled her eyes.

"Hi, Bobby," she said in a low and irritated tone.

"I know you girls are going through a lot. I just want you to know I'm here for you and anything you need. You know I loved your mother. If you need anything, don't hesitate to ask."

"And exactly what the fuck can you do for us from jail? Couldn't do shit all these years for your son, and when Pam got sick, you couldn't do shit then. Damn sure can't do nothing now. The funeral's all paid for. We good over here," Glo said through piercing lips.

Bobby's belted chuckle brought chills to my body. The last thing I wanted was a full-on screaming match between Glo and Bobby in front of the funeral director. Embarrassed for our family, I interjected.

"C'mon Glo, don't do that. Now is not the time for all of this."

"Exactly, Joi. Now is not the time nor place for this jail bird ass nigga to even be a part of this discussion. Give him the address later."

Swiftly, Gloria reached over to me, snatched my phone, and ended the call.

"Gloria. Give me my fucking phone," I said before yanking it from her hand.

"You got this nigga on the phone like he holds any rank to be making any decisions. Pam is our mother, and she left me in charge! He better hope he even get approved to come. Now let's carry the fuck on."

"He is her legal husband. He can very well get approved to attend this funeral. What the fuck is wrong with you?"

"Not if I don't want him there. I don't want nobody dressed in no jail uniform attending my mother's funeral. This ain't that kind of party, gangster," Gloria snarled sarcastically.

On guard, I was instantly offended and got defensive. This was how she felt about all inmates.

Leave it to a bitch who never did no time to be all cold-hearted.

The funeral director sat patiently yet unamused, hoping to display a neutral disposition, perhaps even show that he was not listening, prying, or being nosy, which I appreciated.

Annoyed, I stood up from my chair and slowly pushed it back in its position. Looking at the funeral director, I said, "It looks like not much of me is needed here. Thank you so much. I'll see you next week for the first day of service."

I made my way to the door when Gloria said, "Wait, Joi. I'll only be a few minutes."

"Wait on your fucking cab, Gloria Maxine," I spat back before storming out of the office between the swinging door.

CHAPTER 28

GIGOLO

a man supported by a woman, usually in return for his attentions, a professional dancing partner or male escort.

"Yuh nuh wait pon yuh sister dem?"

This had to be the third time Tony asked me that. I thought if I ignored him the first two times, he would drop it. I was wrong.

"No. Fuck that bitch. Just drive!"

I was so irritated. It was nice hearing Bobby's voice. Why the fuck did Glo have to hang up the phone? She was so fucking selfish. I wanted Bobby to attend Pam's funeral because I knew that's what she would have wanted. For Christ's sake, Bobby was our legal stepfather and Pam's legal husband. What was Glo thinking? He was the closest thing left to Pam. They talked every day on the phone, and they wrote letters to each other twice a week.

So slumped in a daze, I didn't notice Tony call my name. I only snapped out of my daydream once he grabbed my thigh.

"Wea tuh, Princess?"

"Tone, I need some money. Shit not going right, and my sister leaving me high and dry."

Tony remained quiet, which came as a surprise to me. He never had a problem with me asking for money. Most of the time, he offered and splurged. The whole week I was locked up, he laced my commissary with at least five hundred dollars.

We rode in silence for the next few blocks down Fulton Street. As soon as we turned the corner of Classon and passed Franklin, Tony pulled over to the corner in front of a deli.

He put his gear in park and dug in his pocket, pulling out a debit card from his wallet.

"How much yuh need, babes?"

"If you can spare three hundred dollars. If not babes, I'll take two hundred dollars."

Without saying a word, Tony jumped out of the car and headed into the store. Within two silent minutes in his new Cadillac Escalade, a vibrant ping started to go off. I ignored it, but then it vibrated again and again. I rolled down the tinted windows to peer in the store, where I saw Tony standing in the register line with three people in front of him.

Should I look? Do I have enough time? What do I really have to worry about? I knew the worst of it all — that he was married. What else could there be?

I took a deep breath before picking up his red Razr cell phone. As soon as it was in my hands, the vibrating stopped. The screen read four missed calls and two text messages. To my surprise, the phone was unlocked. Nervously, I scurried over to the call log and saw that the four missed calls were from someone named Ann. As I browsed the call log, every entry was saved as a different name. It read as follows:

Ann 1:12pm

Leslie 12:46pm
Gillian 12:12pm
Mariah 11:58am
Celeste 10:32am
Adrienne 10:15am
Beatrice 10:02 am
Dawn 9:47am
Sharlene 9:21am
Tasha 8:47am
Fiona 8:12am

UTTERLY FLABBERGASTED, my jaw dropped. There was no way that between work, me, his wife, and kids he would have time to juggle all of these women. Over the last few months, Tony and I had spent a lot of time together, so if he was seeing these other women, they sure weren't getting much 'cause he was giving me practically all of his time and a large portion of his money. Puzzled, I opened up his text messages. A quick vertical scan of the messages revealed at least five of the same names in the call log.

I clicked on the text message that read *Ann* to find a photo of Tony laying comfortably in a king-sized bed with his favorite fishnet mesh wife beater on. The text message read, *I miss you baby. See you soon.* She made sure to accent the text with a kissy face emoji.

I had been through enough heartbreak. Dealing with different women was the least of my concern. How was I supposed to expect a married man to be faithful to me? In fact, considering what I was going through, being in a relationship was the last thing on my mind. I had a funeral to attend and a daughter to get back on track. My only concern was getting my needs met, not who else this married man was seeing.

After mulling over Ann's text at least three times, I glanced to my right and saw Tony exiting the store and making his way back to the car. Startled, I fumbled to connect his cell phone to the car charger.

Although I tried to play cool, subconsciously, I felt myself getting hot and irritated.

As soon as Tony got in the car, he handed me the three hundred dollars. I couldn't compose my anger, so I snatched the money from him aggressively and sunk back into the car seat. He didn't catch on, so he just continued to drive up Fulton Street. We reached Kingston Avenue in utter silence before Tony attempted to break the ice.

"Babes. Yuh gud? Wea yuh wan me fuh drop yuh? Mi af gwan step owt inna streets fuh ah few likkle runs."

I folded my arms and tightened the grimace on my face. I so badly didn't want to be angry with him, but I couldn't help it.

"Where? To see one of the ten bitches in your call log?"

Without any hesitation, Tony responded,

"Yea, mi gwan pick up mi likkle allowance from tree ov mi gal. Nuh worry, Joi. Mi see yuh later fuh dinner. Mi find anotha spot owt in Queens. Mi wan fuh forward yuh dea."

"Allowance? What the fuck? Shit, I knew you was married, but all these women is too much for me. I'm a one man woman. My ex-man wifed me up. I can't be out here playing with you, and you married with ten side bitches. Not me, playboy. You got the wrong one."

"Listen baby love, tis ting a likkle tew much fuh mi too, gal. Mi running all ova di place — tew jail fuh see yuh, getting in de middle ov yuh an yuh sista dem, buying weteva yu need. Gal, wea yuh tink money ah run from? Di tree? Di ocean? No, gal. Yuh is lucky fuh all of dem wooman — trust dem finance yuh."

The audacity of him.

"So, that's what you do? Hustle women? You need ten of them just to take care of you and those bastards in Jamaica? How pitiful!"

"Yuh suh. Mi call it cockpensation. Every wooman affi pay. Mi should af charged yuh, but mi tew brite suh."

Livid, I waved my hand erratically, signaling for him to stop on the nearest corner of Rockaway and Fulton Street.

"Well, since your bum ass so pressed up for every dollar, keep it," I responded as I threw the three hundred dollars at him. The twenty-dollar bills slapped his face while some fell out of the window as I hopped out of the car so fast and slammed his door.

Who the fuck he think he talking to? My ex took care of me and my daughter. I'd be damned if I played side chick to a married man who needs ten other women so he can afford to be with me. Not when I had someone on speed dial who would simply ask "How high?" after telling him to jump. Mr. Tony Skank truly had me fucked up.

CHAPTER 29

SUPPORT

a thing that bears the weight of something or keeps it upright. Gives assistance to, especially financially; enable to function or act.

I let my emotions get the best of me during a time when I should have been levelheaded, but I didn't care. Just when I thought Tony and I were actually building something; he showed his true colors. To think that I really believed I was the only one made me sick to my stomach. Was I really that naive?

One thing was for sure, I was broke! My stomach growled loudly as I trucked down the hill on Rockaway Avenue towards the block of my apartment with only twenty-six dollars to my name.

I need some money, and I need it fast.

Instead of heading upstairs, I hopped into my car once I made it to my block. I might have been broke, but— a visit to the right person would change all of that very quickly.

I sped off, making my way towards Kingsboro Houses in search of someone who everyone called Pa-Ha due to his notorious paws he laid on many from his street boxing days. Nia and I called him Clyde.

* * *

Beep! Beep!

Two honks were enough to get the attention of the crowd surrounding the corner store on Dean and Rochester. A young cat I recognized, once he turned around and spotted me, made his way towards my car. I rolled down the window about a quarter way down.

"Hey, playboy. You seen Pa-Ha?"

"Yeah, Yeah, Yeah, Yeah. Pa-Pa-Paw Ha he-he-he around the corner. G-G-G Give me a min-in-in ute, le-le-let me get him."

His stark, sickening stutter depressed me.

"Thanks."

I sat patiently, anticipating exactly how I'd deal with Clyde once I saw him. We hadn't seen each other or spoken since Nia's graduation nearly six months ago. Disappointment filled my soul just knowing that yet again, I needed him. I didn't know which hurt more — coming to the realization that I needed him or knowing that ultimately, he would come through in a way that no one else would or could.

Within a few minutes, Clyde turned the corner wearing a Green Nautica jacket tagged with red and yellow patches. His be-bop walk was still reminiscent of the early nineties as he made his way through the corner boy crowd and dabbed up the six hoodlums.

"Pa-Ha," the crowd said in unison as he walked towards my direction. His smile turned to a sad, sullen grimace once he locked eyes with me through the glass window. His circular frames didn't do too bad of a job at attempting to mask his expression. But ultimately, he couldn't hide from me, and I couldn't hide from him.

Clyde walked around to the passenger side and opened the door before he settled in the seat. For the first few minutes, I remained quiet. I couldn't believe I was there.

"Joyce, wassup?"

"Where the fuck do I begin? I got locked up on some probation shit and within a week, Pam died in a nursing home. Me and Glo at odds now. She turned my own baby against me."

Unknowingly, the tears just started to flow until my face was completely drenched from sobbing.

Clyde instantly pulled me closer and hugged me with his left hand that was permanently clenched like a claw, one of the rare deformities I inflicted from a fight we had years ago.

Wow, we really been through the ringer.

"I'm so sorry, Joi. My condolences. You know Pam was my girl. Used to let me bag up in the crib when you was locked up, all'lat. Pam was so thorough but so proper. How's Bobby taking the news up north?" he inquired.

"I don't even know. He called yesterday while we were at the funeral parlor, but Glo hung up on him before we could even really talk. I'm hoping he call back today, but fuck all that. I'm stressed and need some money. Lost my job while locked up, came home to bills out the ass."

"I got you, Joi." Clyde dug in his pocket and pulled out a wad of cash. As he began to count out five one hundred-dollar bills, it dawned on me.

"Nah, I'm talking some bigger money. Look, I got an idea. Take a ride with me."

An hour and a half later, I found a discreet parking spot directly across from the building that allowed us to see but not be seen. The front door was in plain sight, making it easy to identify the key players. Clyde sparked a blunt and passed it to me. I took a long pull, happy to free my mind from the bullshit.

"Look, here he comes," I said, urging Clyde's attention to the tall, Hispanic man leaving the building.

"His name is Felix. He's the full charge accountant. Every day, he leaves the building at twenty-five minutes after five o'clock to head to the bank. He keeps the money in a black plastic bag that he hides in a bigger New York Public Library bag. He never has more than fifteen thousand cash on him, but that's all I need — just a little something to get me out of this hole. We can buss it down fifty-fifty, evenly. Let him walk two blocks down to East 138th before you catch him. I'll meet you on the corner of 138th and Grand Concourse at

5:35. Please don't fuck this up. Neither one of us can afford to go to jail."

"C'mon, Joi. Do I ever fuck up a jook?"

* * *

AFTER I DROPPED CLYDE OFF, I made up my mind that enough was enough, and Nia was coming home with me whether she liked it or not. I was her mother and legal guardian! By the time I made it to Gloria's, the night blue sky was already settled. Unaware of the exact time, but expecting someone to be home, it came to my surprise that after five minutes of knocking, no one answered. I pulled out my cell phone and dialed Gloria. It went straight to voicemail.

This is getting out of hand now. Where the fuck is she with my daughter? I should have never let Nia stay here.

Panicking, I walked towards the hallway window and looked down to the parking lot. Everything around me was crumbling. My mother was gone. My relationship with my daughter was deteriorating day by day, and what I thought was getting better with my sister just took a turn for the worse. When I thought I found a friend and lover in Tony, he showed me that I was wrong.

As much as it hurt to admit it, all I really had was Clyde. Just like Pam, in my time of need, Clyde always came through without questions or judgments. To even feel this way about Clyde was conflicting. Yes, I hated him for what he did to Nia, but I also loved him for helping me raise another man's child. I didn't exactly forgive him; I just numbed my feelings to get my needs met, which would ultimately help me and Nia.

A vibrating sensation on my hip interrupted my thoughts, which caused me to jump back from the window. I fumbled through my bag to grab my phone quickly before it hung up.

"Hello?" I answered

"You have a call from an inmate at Bedford Hills Correctional Facility. Please hold."

"Hello, Joi? Are you there?"

"Yes, Bobby I'm here. I'm sorry about yesterday. Ain't much change. Glo is still a bitch."

"You got that right. Same ole same ole. You always were my favorite. The realest. You know a little something about life. Gloria was spoiled while you took care of her, Pam and my son. I'll forever thank you for that. But how are you holding up?"

"I'm tryna manage, but I'm all alone out here. I ain't even got my daughter right now. Glo done turned Nia against me. I'm outside the apartment now to get Nia and nobody answering. They ain't here. Tryna figure out where the fuck they at."

"How old is Nia again?" he asked.

"She's twelve."

"Yeah, that's old enough to understand loyalty. No matter what, you never turn on your mother."

"C'mon ,Bobby. She's a fucking kid, and Gloria is the one causing the riff between us."

"I know, I know, Joi. Trust, Glo gon' get hers. You don't turn somebody kid against them. But I ain't understanding how Nia fell for that. You were locked up for like a week. Ain't like Glo raised her."

"I know. But don't worry, I'll be alright. Look, the viewing is next Wednesday, starting at three, and the funeral is Thursday morning at eleven. Address is 467 Pacific Street, at the corner of Classon. Let me know if it's approved."

"Trust, baby girl, I'll be there. Just hold ya head."

"Joi."

"Yeah, Bobby?" I answered back.

"How's my son doing? He stopped answering my calls about a year ago. When he first got to college we talked at least twice a week."

"He hasn't gotten into town yet for the funeral. His bus is coming in tonight but he's as good as he could be considering the sudden death of his mother while in college. This shit hit us all bad but I know for him it's hitting the worse- he's only twenty-one you know. This the time you need your mom the most..."

CHAPTER 30

REDEMPTION

the action of saving or being saved from sin, error, or evil. The action of regaining or gaining possession of something in exchange for payment or clearing a debt.

It was twenty minutes after five, as I watched Clyde's shadow disappear from my immediate view. I had just enough time to circle the block past the traffic jam congestion on Fordham Road to meet Clyde exactly at 5:35 on the corner of East 138th Street and Grand Concourse. I parked about three minutes from the building, so that by the time Clyde made it in front, the accountant would be exiting.

I looked down at my digital watch and waited until 5:23 to start my car. With a light pedal on the gas, I slowly drove to the intersection where the building stood. As I signaled left to turn, out the corner of my eye, I saw Clyde swing in a quick motion, and punched Felix in the face . Once I turned the block, I was met with a red light, and now the view was behind me.

As I adjusted my front mirror to lean in, I saw Clyde snatch the bag from the accountant and dart in the opposite direction. He had only seven blocks to run. I knew the accountant wouldn't risk his life and run after Clyde. By the time he would make it back upstairs to report it to the company and call the police, we would be long gone.

The red light turned green, and I sped off down Grand Concourse to East 138th Street. The five minutes it took me to get there felt like forever. The Bronx was normally lively with loud music, the bustle from the 4 train, and the busy shopping strip full of customers. On a normal day, beating this traffic in only five minutes was a blessing, but today it was nerve-racking. I counted every second I sat at a light or at a standstill.

I cannot afford to get caught up for this. I just need a little something to get through. God, please forgive me and protect me.

When I made it in front of the corner store on 138th and Grand Concourse, Clyde was standing by a payphone with the headset to his ear. I honked the horn to get his attention. To my surprise, he disappeared into the store and returned with the New York Public Library bag.

I rolled down my window and yelled, "Hurry up, man!"

As soon as he jumped in the car, I sped off past the red light. It was too hot, and it was time to make my way towards the Major Deegan.

* * *

Clyde insisted that I take him home to get something before we headed back to my crib to count up the bread. Nia was still by Gloria's, so I figured this was the perfect time to get him in and out. Clyde left the New York Public Library bag on the floor of the passenger seat while he ran upstairs in his apartment building. I opened the bag and saw three neatly stacks of one hundred-dollar bills.

Don't look like much, but it'll be enough.

When Clyde appeared back downstairs, he had an overnight duffle bag with him. I didn't hold anything back once he got in the car.

"Uhh, Clyde, thanks, but it ain't that kind of party. I ain't tryna fuck you. We is not on that timing."

"Joi, I know. Look, I ain't even tryna come back to y'all place. I counted it in the store. Like you said, a little under fifteen thousand. It's fourteen thousand, five hundred in there. But this duffle bag got another forty thousand in it. It's all for you. Go buy a house, go do something, whatever you wanna do."

I was so confused. Where the fuck did Clyde *get all this money from?*

"Should I get the fuck out of town? This blood money or something?"

"This money I been saving up for the last two years for us. I was gonna surprise you with it soon. The night before Nia's graduation, after I re-upped, I reached my thirty thousand mark. I was happy and feeling myself, Joi, and I relapsed. I took a hit of crack, and I was fucked up. I came in the house all paranoid, trying to hide it from you. When you asked me to check on Nia, I stayed in her room a little longer than normal to get myself together. I was mad I had fucked up, and I felt the demon taking over my mind. I started crying so hard. The guilt from relapsing had me do the unthinkable, to violate a child I raised. I'm so sorry, Joi. I just want you to know nothing more than touching happened."

I was at a loss for words. My eyes were red and filled with water from conflicting emotions of surprise and annoyance.

"Clyde, why the fuck did you go through with the robbery if you had it to help me out?"

Clyde smirked and said, "Because it was just like old times. When you came by with a plan just like a No Limit solider, I followed suit."

I rolled my eyes and sucked my teeth. Clyde could see my irritation. I wondered if he could also see my gratitude.

"Just take the money, Joi. I want you to have it."

Before I could say thank you, Clyde leaned over and kissed me on the cheek. He got out of the car without saying another word and began walking. Once he hit the corner, he turned and vanished from my sight.

* * *

I WAS IN TOTAL SHOCK. I did not expect to walk away with nearly sixty thousand dollars. This was enough money to move out of state, put a down payment on a house, and still save a little extra for Nia's college fund. I had some decent skills and could get a job to hold me over. Although I had to hook a crook to get the first fifteen thousand, I lifted my head, closed my eyes, and worshipped God.

"Thank you, Jesus. Thank you, Jesus. Thank you, Jesus."

I glanced down at the rack of hangers I had in my hand and knew I'd be in Macy's a bit longer. I had to get Nia and me something nice to wear for Pam's funeral. I had even thought about buying Glo, her son, and our brother matching colors to wear like old times when I shopped and stole for all of them. However, considering that Glo had received Pam's insurance money, I figured she was good. I wouldn't dare overstep and spend my money on an outfit for her son to tell me he's not going to wear it. Secondly, my brother was twenty-one and he was old enough to dress himself. Besides, since Glo always bragged about the fact that our brother lived with her and visited me, I figured she wouldn't have a problem holding down baby bro and making sure he looked good for Pam's last day.

To avoid arriving at Glo's with no one there, I dialed her house phone. Surprisingly, she answered on the first ring.

"Glo, I'm in the city shopping. I'll be at the house in about an hour."

"Cool, see you soon. Nia's here too."

This was by far the most relaxed exchange I had with Glo in a while. Sounded like she was happy, and I sure was too.

When I got to Gloria's house, I only brought the three bags of clothes I bought for Nia upstairs with me. I could tell my baby was in need of a new wardrobe from the time she visited me in Rikers. Although, I was still hurt that Nia teamed up with Glo to fight me, I had to just let it go. Families fight and Nia and Glo are all I have. I didn't want to bring it up while Glo was around but as soon as the funeral was over and Nia was back at home with me, I would address it. Now, I just had to remain cool.

As soon as Nia saw me enter the apartment with shopping bags, her face lit up. It had been a long time since I'd seen a smile on my baby's face that I put there.

I just wanted my baby back. I was ready and willing to put everything behind us —. All I wanted was my baby back in my presence so I could reprogram her.

"Baby, come look at what I got you. Some cute sweater dresses, some wool tights, and True Religion jeans for school," I said as I pulled out the items from the bag and unfolded them for display.

Gloria was sitting on a stool filing her nail. She was awfully quiet as she sat with a straight face, watching every move I made.

"This is your outfit for the funeral." I unzipped the black garment bag to reveal a beautiful, black, quarter-length dress, accented with pink and white polka dots near the bottom and the collar.

That was when Gloria got up from the bar stool and walked closer to us. I pulled the dress off of the hanger and handed it to Nia.

"Go try it on," I urged.

"The colors for the family are sage, white, and silver to match Pam's casket. Also, green was her favorite color. I already got matching outfits for Nia and my baby. If you want to join in with the colors, you're more than welcome to."

"When did you decide the colors of the funeral?"

"The day you left the funeral home, upset after Bobby called."

"That was four days ago. Why the fuck didn't you tell me?"

"Slipped my mind. You might as well return Nia's outfit and just exchange what you bought for yourself and get something sage and white."

"Enough is enough with these charades. I'm taking my daughter home. C'mon Nia, get your bookbag and leave everything else. We getting outta here."

I started folding the clothes and putting them back in the bag before I noticed that Nia hadn't moved.

"Nia, go get your school bag and let's go NOW."

Nia stood defiantly and turned her gaze to Gloria.

"Go do what your mother says. It's best you go home with your mom. I could use a break."

"Auntie, I don't want to go."

Annoyed, hurt, and irritated, I couldn't believe my ears.

"You don't have no fucking choice, Nia. Now let's go."

This time, I did not wait for her to move. I yanked her by the arm and walked her towards the back room where she stayed.

"Let's go now."

Nia took her time, slow dragging. She grabbed a duffle bag and began throwing clothes and books inside.

"Leave all that shit. Just bring ya coat and yaself. Now!"

CHAPTER 31

LOYALTY

the state or quality of being loyal; faithfulness to commitments or obligations, faithful adherence to a sovereign, government, leader, cause, etc. An example or instance of faithfulness, adherence, or the like.

Sage wasn't a bad color for a casket. It actually looked quite nice — soft, yet rich in hue at the same time. I was happy I changed my mind and decided to go with the color coordination Gloria chose. It wasn't worth the trouble of arguing or fighting any longer. Pam was gone, and the damage was already done. Instead of contesting, I just went along to get along.

All five of us — me, Nia, Glo, her son, and our little brother wore sage with an accent of white and silver. The richness of the sage against our chocolate skin tones made us stand out amongst the hundreds of white magnolias and snap dragons spread throughout the funeral home.

With an expectation of at least one hundred attendees, double the amount of yesterday's viewing, I was shocked to find that we were the only ones there by 10:15 am. We trickled our way down the aisle to the altar, one by one, with Gloria leading the way to take one last look at Pam before a crowd arrived.

Gloria, dressed in a mid-length, form-fitting sage bodycon dress with silver four-inch strappy heels, approached the opening of the casket, leaned over and planted a long, warm kiss on Pam's forehead. Although I couldn't make out any of her words, I saw Gloria's lips moving while planted on her. Glo remained crouched down with her lips still on Pam and tears in her eyes. After about three minutes, she switched places with her son.

"Fly Guy, tell your grandmother how much you gon' miss her. Tell her goodbye."

Her son, who was about a year and half younger than Nia at ten years old, stood shyly behind her before approaching and saying,

"I miss you so much already, grandma."

Gloria grabbed him by the hand and moved to the side to take her seat in the front row.

Nia stood confidently next to me, aware of the permanence of this event. Although I conformed to the dress colors, I did, however, exchange the dress Gloria bought for her to a selection of my choice. I chose a sage, chiffon, quarter-length dress with a white and silver bow cinched at the waist for Nia. I, dressed in a sage, chiffon halter top pant suit, touched the small of Nia's back, encouraging her to walk with me as I approached the casket.

Pam's lifeless body laid so gracefully and peacefully in her heavenly eternal bed. She looked so good. The morticians did a great job with her makeup, matching her tone perfectly with a dewy finished look rather than a dead Casper glow. Her lips were pursed with the classic red lipstick she always wore.

She wore a short, honey blonde bob wig with bangs that framed her face beautifully. Her nail color matched her white suit with a touch of sage for the color of the casket. I smiled down at her in amusement. I refused to be sad. Today was the day the Lord hath made and most importantly, the day we welcomed her home to Him.

Although I was sad to lose Pam, I was grateful that I had my mother for the first thirty-one years of my life and thankful she got to meet her first grandchild, Nia. As I leaned over to kiss her, I heard a trickle of footsteps and voices enter the sanctuary. People were starting to arrive. Nia said her goodbyes, and I grabbed her by the hand as we took our seats in the front row, opposite of the section where Gloria sat.

Glo made it clear yesterday at the viewing that she did not want to sit near our father or Bobby. She was still holding a grudge against our father for moving down south when we were teenagers, and most recently, for not checking on Pam or us while she was in the nursing home. So, I decided I would sit with Daddy while she sat with our little brother, who really needed support. Bobby was locked up for most of our brother's life — about fifteen years out of nineteen. Our brother had only seen his father during prison visits.

A few years back when my brother was in high school, Pam made a big fuss about him changing his last name to match Bobby's. Literally up until he turned fifteen, my brother had my father's last name because during the time Pam gave birth, she still went by Pamela Holloway. She had spent all of her adult life as a Holloway and didn't find it necessary to drop the last name just because they were divorced. It wasn't until a few years into Bobby's bid that they actually got married. At that time, immediately changing our brother's last name was not a pressing matter until it became one.

My phone vibrated and I looked down to see a text message from Clyde that read, "I'm outside; 'bout to come walk in. I'll sit in the back. Just want to pay my respects."

I responded with, "Okay."

So much for being discreet. Nia spotted Clyde as soon as he entered the funeral home. Not sure what prompted her to turn around, but she caught wind of him fast. Appalled, she turned to me with a disgusted look and asked, "What is he doing here?"

I hadn't told Nia about the money Clyde gave me and that I had three houses I was looking at in Atlanta. She didn't need to know everything. She was a child.

"Nia, he came to show his respects, and he'll be leaving."

"Why would you invite him here?"

Irritated by the questions, I lied and said, "I didn't invite him. He found out from Bobby, your uncle's father. They're friends and stay in touch."

I just wanted her to be quiet, and I wanted service to begin so it could end. To my surprise, Nia jumped out of her seat, grabbed her small clutch, and moved to the opposite side. There were at least twenty-five people present as more came into the funeral home. Unaware of our exchange, Gloria was just as shocked when Nia angrily sat down next to her. After sitting down, Nia turned around and pointed to Clyde. Glo held her head back in defeat and cut me a darting look. I just rolled my eyes.

I was so busy watching Nia and Glo across from me and simultaneously keeping an eye on Clyde in the back, I didn't notice Daddy walking down the aisle. I felt a warm touch on my shoulder. I turned around to see Daddy standing tall and firm, dressed in a sage linen suit and cowboy boots that were white with a touch of green and blue painted on the sides.

"Hey, baby girl. How you holding up?" Daddy asked before leaning over to kiss my cheek.

"I'm hanging in there. Thank you so much for being here both days, Daddy. Where's Louise?" I pondered.

"I asked her to stay at the hotel today. She didn't know I'd be delivering the eulogy, and I just didn't want any drama on Pam's last day. Where's my grandbaby?"

"Sitting over there by her aunt," I said as I nodded my head to the right in their direction.

Daddy sighed and took off his hat, revealing his bald head, and sat down. He shook his head from side to side.

"Nothing has changed. From little girls, you two have always been at each other's throats."

He was right. Glo and I had always been at it. I avoided responding to my dad's comment and took a look around the room.

"Gosh, I ain't know Pam was still in touch with some of the same people we met in rehab before you girls were born."

Daddy pulled out his sunglasses case, opened it, and threw on his black shades.

I couldn't help but laugh at my dad's facial expression. Until he pointed it out, I wouldn't have recognized many of them. Truth was, my parents were real addicts that met in rehab and kicked dope. They were clean for years until the eighties came and the crack epidemic happened and hooked them again. Having parents as drug users, I always stayed away from anything other than weed.

As I scanned the room, I noticed that Nia was sitting next to Gloria's son. Neither Gloria nor my little brother were in sight. I glanced down at my watch and saw that it was 10:45am. Service was set to start in fifteen minutes. Luckily, before I made it out of my seat, I heard the shackles and the commotion.

Daddy looked at me inquisitively and raised his eyebrow.

"Baby girl, go see what's going on over there."

As soon as I stood up and turned around, I could see Gloria and our brother standing face to face with his father, Bobby.

Dressed in full inmate gear — an orange jail jumpsuit — and escorted by correctional officers, Bobby stood a little over six feet tall. It had been years since I'd seen him in the flesh. He wasn't my Daddy, so I didn't visit him frequently. Out of the last fifteen years, I'd seen him maybe three times while accompanying Pam and my little brother.

The curse words became clearer as I got closer to the lobby of the parlor, approaching the scene. My brother stood behind Glo as she inched closer and closer to Bobby, who had not even been released from his shackles yet.

"Ma'am, can you please lower your voice and refrain from getting too close? Please allow us to escort the inmate to his seat," one of the guards warned.

"I don't even know why he's here. He's a fucking deadbeat. A deadbeat husband. A deadbeat father and a deadbeat stepfather. Just like you to show up when it's all over," Glo barked.

By now, the entire room full of attendees were turned around and gawking at us. Determined to diffuse the situation, I stepped in.

"Glo, just chill. Let him take a seat. Don't embarrass us in front of these people on Pam's last day." I reached for her arm gently, and she slapped my hand away.

"Man, fuck these people. This nigga in a jail uniform with handcuffs on. It doesn't get any more embarrassing than that."

"Glo, lower your voice and relax. Just squash it. We about to get started in a few minutes."

"Joi, mind your business and sit down. This is between me and my bitch ass father, who was never here. You had your father. Go talk to him. Stay out of this." I was startled to hear my brother speak.

"Little boy, I raised you. Don't you dare bass up at me."

"Oh please, Joyce-Ann, fuck you. We all know I raised him. Instead of worrying about him, you need to be worried about this fucking pedophile that touched your daughter, hiding out in the back like nobody sees him. His ass needs to be in cuffs too."

Right before four correctional officers began moving Bobby swiftly into the room where the funeral was being held, he turned to me and said, "Joi, go sit. Don't worry. She can't argue alone."

Aggravated, Gloria yelled out, "Jailbird, deadbeat ass nigga."

Not only was Clyde standing and scoping out the situation, but Nia also scurried past the crowd and was standing a few feet behind Gloria and my brother.

"Glo, calm down, please. We got old folks in here — people who really loved Pam. We can't be in here showing our ass. Just let it go. Today is about celebrating our mother's legacy."

Gloria was steaming with passion, and she just wouldn't let it rest.

"So, you on this nigga side? He coming in here tryna act like daddy and husband of the year, knowing damn well he been locked up for his son's entire life. Spare me the phony bullshit."

Angrily, she pulled her small pocketbook off of her shoulder, rummaged through it, and pulled out her cell phone.

"Man, fuck all of y'all. I'll be back. I'm going outside to make a call." She turned around quickly and headed towards the exit door.

"Auntie, I wanna come with you," Nia yelled as Gloria neared the exit.

"Well, hurry up."

"Nia, come here. You ain't going nowhere!" I screamed as I walked closer to the door. Gloria was already outside.

"Ma, I want to talk to Auntie just for a minute."

What the heck? We should be getting started soon.

Through clenched teeth, I turned to Nia and said, "Fine. Be back here in five minutes."

With Gloria out of the way momentarily, I made a loud announcement to the funeral home, apologizing for the loud outburst. I walked to Clyde, who was still standing near the last row of seating, and shook my head.

"Since I've known you, Joi, Glo has always been a hot head."

I rolled my eyes and proceeded to continue walking towards the front row, where Bobby sat on the corner seat surrounded by two correctional officers. The other two stepped outside moments before Gloria to patrol the outside of the funeral home. I walked over to Bobby, leaned over, and kissed him on the cheek.

"Thank you so much for coming, and I'm sorry about Gloria."

He shook his head unbothered and said, "It's a tense time. I understand. We all miss Pam."

I nodded in agreement and turned to the second row where Daddy was sitting.

"You remember my father, right?" I asked Bobby as I turned around to include Daddy in the conversation.

"Yeah, I remember your dad. Only met him once."

Just when Daddy reached out his hand to shake Bobby's, a loud thump startled me. Within seconds, I heard another thump, then a crack, and the sound of glass shattering.

All I could hear was Clyde's voice yelling, "Get down, Joi! Get down!"

The forty or so people there were more confused than panicky. Some of them were already on the floor while others were still sitting upright. My brother sat in the opposite row, holding Gloria's son tightly to him.

"Stay right there. Let me find out what's going on," I warned my brother.

As I began to walk towards the door, I saw the two correctional officers from outside rush back in the building past me to the room where the attendees sat.

"Let's go! Let's go! We've got to escort the inmate back to the facility," the tall Latino officer yelled to his colleagues, who were overseeing Bobby.

"What's going on?" I asked.

"Ma'am, there's been a shooting."

"A shooting?" I questioned.

Without receiving confirmation, I pushed open the door to the sidewalk, where drops of blood trailed from the concrete to the smooth road in the street. Then the panic came over me.

"Where's Nia? Where's my baby at? NIA! NIA!" I screamed.

I felt Clyde touch my shoulder. Although I didn't turn around to him and I couldn't hear a thing, I could discern his touch from anywhere at any time.

I felt my body lose oxygen as all the air disappeared from my breath.

It was sunny but awfully cold out, so I didn't feel the ripping wind when I ran in the middle of the street, where Gloria laid discombobulated with blood seeping from the gunshot wound in the middle of her head. Her mouth and eyes were open, and I could already tell she was gone from her emotionless stare. The anguish began to fester in my heart and before I knew it, I was on my knees next to her, crying hysterically.

"Jesus. Why? How could you do this? My mother, my sister? How?"

Tears continued to flow as they dropped on Gloria's lifeless face. She didn't blink or move an inch. Overwhelmed by witnessing my sister's demise, it didn't hit me until a minute later that I still had no idea where Nia was.

I wiped my tears, planted a long kiss on Gloria's cheek, then raised my body up from the ground. As soon as I got up and looked back towards the building, I saw a crowd of people outside the funeral home making way for others to exit.

"NIA! NIA!" I screamed again and again as I paced up and down.

The most devastating sight stood before my eyes. Nia couldn't hear me because she was buried facedown behind a gray SUV.

"Nia baby, Nia, it's your Mommy. Wake up. Wake up!" I said frantically as I shook her body. There were four, fresh piercing bullet holes in her back. Once I rolled her over, her eyes were closed shut.

"Oh, Jesus. Not my baby. Not my baby too. Not my baby! Please tell me this is a dream, Jesus. Please wake me up!"

I held Nia in my arms so tight that I didn't even feel my brother try to pick me up from the ground. I turned around and saw the tears in his eyes as well. He embraced me tightly, and we stood there crying until we were interrupted by Bobby being escorted out into his van by the correctional officers.

"Can I say goodbye to my son quickly?" Bobby asked his officer.

The officer nodded his head. "You've got two minutes, inmate. The cops are on their way to address this matter, but we gotta get you outta here. Hurry up."

"Sure thing, I'll be quick."

Bobby inched closer to us while the officers stepped a few feet back to demonstrate privacy. My brother pulled away from my embrace.

"You lucky you my son so let me give you this very valuable piece of advice. Never turn on the people who've made sure you were good. Remember, loyalty is everything."

Bobby's voice was so low and intense as he pointed his index finger in the middle of his son's head. My brother stood weak and shaken with a tight lip.

I quickly darted my eyes at Bobby in disbelief and disgust.

"Joi, hold ya head."

At that very moment, that was all I could do — wrap my head around the madness that was now my reality.

"Auntieeeeeeeeeee!"

I looked up startled to see Gloria's son running towards me. Once near, I grabbed him tightly and rested my head on top of his.

"Don't worry, baby. Auntie got you," I said while fighting back tears. My brother joined the embrace as all three of us stood there, hugging while Bobby jumped into the police van and disappeared in the wind.

THE END

For now...

Join Penny's reader community on Facebook at www.facebook.com/author.pennyblacwrite

LIKE Author Page www.facebook.com/authorpennybwrite.

INSTAGRAM: www.instagram.com/pennyblacwrites

WANT TO BE NOTIFIED WHEN THE NEW, HOT URBAN FICTION AND INTERRACIAL ROMANCE BOOKS ARE RELEASED?

Text the keyword "JWP" to 22828 to receive an email notifying you of new releases, giveaways, announcements, and more!

Jessica Watkins Presents is the home of many well-known, best-selling authors in Urban Fiction and Interracial Romance. We provide editing services, promotion and marketing, one-on-one consulting with a renowned, national best-selling author, assistance in branding, and more, FREE of charge to you, the author.

We are currently accepting submissions for the following genres: Urban Fiction/Romance, Interracial Romance, and Interracial/Paranormal Romance. If you are interested in becoming a best-selling author and have a FINISHED manuscript, please send the synopsis, genre and the first three chapters in a PDF or Word file to jwp.submissions@gmail.com. Complete manuscripts must be at least 45,000 words.Tag a friend or family member who you know needs to be a published author!

Made in the USA
Monee, IL
23 July 2021